Prince Louie

Prince Louie

Catherine's Son

Final Episode to the Devil's Cave Trilogy

John Nuzzolese

Copyright © 2012 by John Nuzzolese.

Library of Congress Control Number: 2012904036
ISBN: Hardcover   978-1-4691-7914-8
                Softcover   978-1-4691-7913-1
                Ebook   978-1-4691-7915-5

All rights reserved. No part of this book may be reproduced or transmitted in any form or by any means, electronic or mechanical, including photocopying, recording, or by any information storage and retrieval system, without permission in writing from the copyright owner.

This is a work of fiction. Names, characters, places and incidents either are the product of the author's imagination or are used fictitiously, and any resemblance to any actual persons, living or dead, events, or locales is entirely coincidental.

This book was printed in the United States of America.

To order additional copies of this book, contact:
Xlibris Corporation
1-888-795-4274
www.Xlibris.com
Orders@Xlibris.com
100231

CONTENTS

Dedication vii
Acknowledgments ix
Introduction xi
Prologue xiii

1. The Beginning 1
2. Reflections 4
3. Quicksand's Reply 7
4. Current Affairs 11
5. Cherbourg 14
6. Point of Contention 17
7. Lafitte's Agenda 20
8. Father and Son Talk 23
9. Gilbert Revisited 26
10. Ray of Sunshine 28
11. Bevier 31
12. Louie Interrupts 34
13. Monsieur Murielle 37
14. Communiqué 39
15. Truffaut's First Revelation 41
16. Charles's Ultimatum 43
17. Truffaut's Final Revelation 45
18. Reunion 48
19. Items of Concern 51
20. Veil of Deceit 54
21. Unexpected Visitor 56

22.	Plot to Kill	58
23.	Charles and Lafitte Part I	61
24.	Charles and Lafitte Part II	64
25.	Charles and Lafitte Part III	66
26.	Charles and Lafitte Part IV	69
27.	Recap of Events	73
28.	Justice Served	76
29.	Change of Plan	79
30.	Clash of Forces	81
31.	Brother to Brother	83
32.	Charles and Henry Part I	85
33.	Charles and Henry Part II	87
34.	Charles and Henry Part III	91
35.	Charles and Henry Part IV	94
36.	Charles and Henry Part V	96
37.	Jacques Lafitte's Dilemma	99
38.	Lafitte and Louie Part I	102
39.	Lafitte and Louie Part II	105
40.	Lafitte and Louie Part III	109

Epilogue	113
Author's Note	117

Dedication

*

For those who serve their Creator in abiding faith, love, and Christmas peace.

Acknowledgments

Gratitude and thanks to

God the Holy Spirit—You are the love of the Father and the Son who gives incentive to God's children in saying no to sin and yes to Him.

Introduction

Prince Louie had been conceived within the palace gardens beneath flowering cherry blossoms and freshly trimmed rose bushes. This particular common act of love exceeded the throes of a deceitful interlude. It was a bond of intimacy that was forged by two lovers whose restless spirits sought human relief and solace in the bloom of irresistible passion. The man, Jacques Lafitte, was a dedicated servant to the king, his dashing treasury minister. The woman, as fate so ordained, happened to be the young princess bride of Charles, Queen Catherine of France.

Ordinarily, an audacious act of this magnitude would condone reprehensible torture preceding one's execution. However, because of extenuating circumstances, after Charles learned the truth of the matter, that Lafitte and Catherine's fleeting affair in the Rose Garden had been somewhat of a godsend, an unanticipated display of emotion enacted in complete secrecy, the king relented in exacting severe punitive measures.

Charles could not find it within himself to admonish his deceased queen's spirit by reeking havoc of revenge against her lover. The last thing he'd wish, for the rest of his days, was to arouse ghostly torments emanating from Catherine's grave rebuking him for his lack of sensitivity in forgiving her this single act of indiscretion. More importantly, however, Jacques Lafitte had been the instrument in siring an heir to the throne of France, a duty Charles, because of his impotency, was incapable to uphold. How safe, he often wondered, was this ominous secret to remain cloistered from public knowledge? The thought incessantly tugged at his consciousness, especially when the illegitimate young prince intermingled in his presence.

As the final tale to the *Devil's Cave* trilogy unfolds, one might reflect in comparing Catherine's legacy to France with the final endowment each of us will pass on to our own precious loved ones. For better for worse, let it be for the better.

Prologue

A mighty treasure had been lost in the early sixteen hundreds. Four centuries later, in a remote burial place along the craggy coast of Maine, its discovery seemingly brought the saga to a definitive conclusion. However, far more intriguing than caskets of trinkets or gold, there remains a curious footnote to the tale that cannot be readily dismissed—namely, the resolution of Catherine's legacy. Had Louie, her illegitimate son, been destined to be Charles's successor to the throne of France?

Sixteen years have passed since Captain Jacques Lafitte set out to sea in a small shore boat to fade into oblivion. It had been apparent to the crew of the *Sea Witch* that it'd be futile to attempt to restrain their captain from taking his own life. So despondent had Jacques been, after witnessing firsthand there was no hope of Catherine's recovery from her stricken condition, for him to go on living became meaningless.

It was during a quiet walk along one of the meandering beaches of an uninhabited island south of Martinique that Lafitte recalled to mind the remarkable occasion of his surrender to utter folly. Refusing to take food or drink with him before Jacques departed from his brethren, less than a week had passed before he succumbed to unconsciousness. Upon being aroused from his stupor, Lafitte recognized a familiar voice.

* * *

"You didn't think we'd actually abandon you, Captain? Under the circumstances, Yates here thought hanging back a safe distance behind your craft was the best thing to do, hoping, of course, you'd soon come to your senses. When the swells began to rise, he couldn't get a proper fix on your coordinates. We thought you were a goner, that maybe the sea swallowed you up or something." Lafitte's quartermaster, Muslim Green, had spoken with a hint of excited relief in his voice.

Yates chimed in, as he paused to feed another spoonful of broth to Lafitte, "Captain, I reckon Quicksand knew what he was doing when the dubious little rascal didn't stop you from paddling away. Isn't that right, mateys?"

Quicksand's voice betrayed his jubilance. "A little time alone was all you needed is what every one of us figured. For a while though, we thought the sharks finished you off. Luckily, the Sea Witch somehow turned itself about, and that's when Patrice's keen eye spotted you. Perhaps John Brough's still watching out for you from above." (It was Captain Brough who intervened in saving Jacques's life during a recent sea battle on the *Vera Cruz* where Catherine was being held hostage by Pierre Fuquay, Lafitte's archenemy.) "No, Quicksand," Jacques recollected, saying in response to what he had just heard, "it wasn't John Brough who pointed the way. Catherine—it was Catherine who led you to me. For some inexplicable reason, my life, at least for now, has been ordained to pursue its miserable course."

1

The Beginning

Jacques Lafitte and his crew had learned that Catherine passed away soon after she arrived in France aboard the king's ship. Reportedly, the queen's voyage to the Caribbean had been overwhelming. Pierre Fuquay's harrowing interrogations, which she never revealed to anyone, had taken its toll. The frightful interlude Catherine encountered with renegade pirates that attacked and looted the *Vera Cruz* of its untold treasures weakened her fragile disposition considerably. The Queen's primary cause of death, however, had been attributed to the premature birth of her son while at sea.

As the *Sea Witch* zigzagged among the islands, Lafitte asked his crew to give serious thought to what he asked them to consider earlier. It was Jacques's utmost desire to return to France. A compelling force seemed to have taken hold of his senses. Although he and his men failed to locate the treasure Charles had mandated them to recover before ever again being allowed to set foot on French soil, Lafitte's yearning for his homeland could not be stilled.

For more than fifteen years, Jacques and his crew searched every conceivable hideaway in the Caribbean where Benitez Chavez, the renegade pirate responsible for taking off with the vast treasure, was likely to have fled. Leaving nothing to chance, Lafitte's ship sailed the northern waters where Chavez had actually traversed. However, not a single trace of his ever being there was duly recorded in Jacques's log.

Pierre Fuquay's execution came as no surprise. He had abused the trust of his king once too often by indulging in nefarious deceptions, including murder and treason. It was a wonder that Charles tarried so long in recognizing his dubious deputy minister's disloyalty. During the same period in question, it was proven beyond all doubt that Jacques Lafitte and his father, Dantes, had been innocent of Fuquay's alleged allegations of high treason. Although the two were officially exonerated in a royal proclamation, Lafitte considered it his duty to fulfill Charles's direct order—to locate the stolen treasure before ever returning to France.

Something Dantes once told him popped into Jacques's recollections. *"Loyalty to one's king goes without question, but we must remember that a king, like the rest of us, is a mere mortal—sometimes fragile, sometimes strong. Either way, you must give him your undying allegiance. However, never feel compelled to follow in the footsteps of a king who is disloyal to his subjects. Forbearance, compassion, tolerance, and justice must precede a monarch's footprints, if indeed they are to be shadowed."* Lafitte wondered, after all that transpired in these past years, which of the two sets of footprints Charles had been engraving upon the sands of time.

Subsequent to the rush of conflicting perplexities parading through his head, Jacques ordered his first mate, Peter La Ruche (Quicksand) to set sail for St. Lucia, a haven that nestled in the vast archipelago along the Lesser Antilles. It is here, amid this pristine shoreline of fruit-bearing trees, exotic birds, and the rhythmic cadence of rippling waves, Captain Lafitte gathered his men under a moonlit sky and disclosed his innermost thoughts.

2

Reflections

While a symphony of indigenous creatures serenaded nature's evening song, Lafitte addressed his mates. He'd speak to them about the compelling forces that prompted him back to France. Perhaps then Jacques's shipmates would have a semblance of meaning to their captain's recent unintelligible spells and strange behavior.

Lafitte had distanced himself from the crew. He'd spend hours alone in his cabin or isolate himself atop the crow's nest, aimlessly staring toward the eastern horizon. It was though Jacques had been entranced, unconscious of everything around him; that is, until he spontaneously awakened from his lethargy and made an announcement that mystified his mates. Beneath a kaleidoscope of stars, Lafitte released the pent-up anxieties that had bound him to a prison of silence. The crew would listen attentively to every word, hoping they'd better understand what caused their captain to bare his soul so suddenly.

Jacques began by invoking Catherine's name. It was her persistent spirit that had been beckoning to him, that aroused Lafitte to reality. He was certain of it. Of course, how could Jacques be so naive? The impact of his sudden premonition had prompted him to clearly see through whatever it was that entangled his subconscious thoughts. Catherine had indeed been reaching out to Lafitte. She was urging her lover back to France. However, try as he may, he didn't know why.

Monsieur Dantes Lafitte came next in the captain's brief soliloquy, for it was he who had given Jacques, then Louie Grapier, a new lease on life. Dantes embraced him at the age of twelve when he stowed away on one of the king's ships, the *Orgueil de France.* It was this kind and loving adventurer who introduced young Louie to the Caribbean. Soon after, he adopted the boy, ingratiating him with a name of great renown. Aside from his birth mother, Leticia, and Catherine, Dantes had instilled in him an unyielding reverence for God.

There were occasions when Pierre Fuquay's image crept into Lafitte's forethoughts. Jacques felt he had to be explained away to his audience. The despot who orchestrated the death of Dantes in the streets of Paris played a crucial role in the events that forged his life. To rehash the entire drama this villainous scoundrel wielded in Lafitte's past appeared senseless. Catherine convinced Jacques to forgive him. Revenge and hatred for Fuquay quickly dissipated, especially when she cautioned Lafitte that neither Catherine nor Jacques could ever achieve eternal bliss together unless their hearts were in accordance with God's merciful forgiveness.

Surprisingly, Charles did grant Lafitte permission to see Catherine and their newborn son for one last time. Although she appeared to be in a deep sleep as he knelt beside her, Jacques perceived that Catherine had been aware of his presence. Moments later, Lafitte's crew had witnessed from the foredeck of the *Sea Witch* Jacques's scourging by Charles's own hand. They now listened intently as he vividly reminded them of the hapless occasion.

The excruciating punishment Jacques Lafitte received was for commandeering Catherine's intended gift to Charles, an unprecedented newly crafted five-mast frigate. The king had vehemently shouted for all to hear, *"Monsieur Lafitte has taken His Majesty's ship without my consent. I gave him ten lashes, as you have all just witnessed, for this indiscretion. As most of you know, France, Spain, and England have lost a wealth of treasure. Monsieur Lafitte and his crew know the waters of the Caribbean far better than any among you. Under the penalty of death, I forbid him to return to France until the looted contraband is recovered."*

"Under the penalty of death" were Charles's exact words. How could Lafitte suggest that his men follow in his footsteps? After expressing gratitude to his shipmates for being his standard-bearers all these years, Jacques concluded, "Gentlemen, I am no longer your captain. The *Sea Witch* is yours. I'm returning to France at my earliest convenience. May God bless you and remain forevermore in your favor."

3

Quicksand's Reply

Moments after Jacques Lafitte concluded his commentary, Quicksand stepped forward. The captain's first mate spoke emphatically. "Each of us can attest that we've been brutalized by the purveyors of social injustice. These pretentious citizens of the republic, while pretending to be patriots, have dared to proclaim us French traitors. I assure you, none here has warranted an ignoble fate such as we've endured all these years."

At the very outset of his utterances, Quicksand struck a chord of solidarity that enlivened the hearts of his shipmates. "We need not be reminded of the unjust indignities chained to our very souls by those in high places who claimed to be friends of the people. However, lest we forget, you shall hear them."

La Ruche cleared his throat. "For the want of a loaf of bread, Patrice was sentenced to the Bastille for three abominable years. To this date, he remains clueless to whatever became of his family. We all know Yates here had been justified in vilifying the state for overtaxing those who least could afford it. Ten years of imprisonment is what the courts gave him, and for what—freedom of speech?"

Lafitte's ears perked up to the orator's soliloquy. "Who among us can ever forget Monsieur Dantes Lafitte? A finer statesman never lived. He, like the rest of us, was maligned and brutally betrayed. His advocacy for change would have made a difference to our beloved country, if only his proclamation of reform and justice for all the classes had been heeded. No, it wasn't to be. Self-righteous proponents of the status quo saw to that."

As though the personal memory he was about to address still clawed at his guts, Peter La Ruche angrily spouted, "The property I inherited had been confiscated by solicitors whom I trusted. After discovering I'd been deceived, my vehement protests were lodged in court. The magistrate at the time, Pierre Fuquay, who undoubtedly had a scheming interest in the matter, deemed me a menace to society. Denying me the privilege of challenging his outrageous decree, he promptly had me locked up in that hellhole of a prison, giving me sufficient reason to ponder whether it would have been better that I'd never been born."

Pausing, Quicksand recanted, "Mateys, it serves little purpose for me to continue. I see it in your faces. We've endured enough pain and sorrow to last a hundred lifetimes. What say ye, comrades? Are you with me? Let's take back what rightfully belongs to us. However, to engage in pagan practices to achieve our end, it would be much the same as sleeping with the enemy. *Our fight*, you've often heard our captain say, *must be fought in the name of truth and justice*."

The crew responded with shouts of "Hear, Hear." Quicksand's voice cracked with emotion when he said, "Jacques, it was you, with the help of God Almighty, who freed us from the bonds of severity and oppression. If you recall, we took an oath to uphold you. The Brotherhood of Dantes Revenge agreed, when we first formed our alliances, that at a time you received full satisfaction for all the injustices transpired against you and your father—it would be regarded a communal exoneration, vindicating each of us as well."

Brandishing his sword, Quicksand spoke resolutely, "There will be no more talk. Action, not words, is the new order of the day." Looking directly at Lafitte, he concluded, "Captain, you have served us well. We hereby reaffirm our pledge to uphold you in fulfilling whatever course of action you choose to follow in the days ahead."

Again excited bellows, "Hear! Hear!" filled the air.

Stroking his whiskers, Quicksand then said, "Captain, it is my utmost displeasure to have to be the one to inform you—and all of us are quite unanimous in this—the Brotherhood of Dantes Revenge hereby charges you with dereliction of duty, a grievous matter that needs to be rectified immediately. You see, the young lad next in line to be King of France needs the strength, wisdom, and courage that stems only from the loins of his true father. Perhaps then he'll have at least a fair chance to reestablish in our homeland the torch of freedom whose smoldering flames need to be rekindled. What say ye, mates?"

A thunderous, "Guilty!" permeated the deck.

As if a sudden bolt of lightning sparked Jacques Lafitte to the threshold of a new dawn, in an instant, all had been made clear to him. "Men," he said, "I acknowledge your reproach with self-indignation and from hereon pledge to rectify my inexcusable negligence of duty. Furthermore, I shall not rest until restitution and justice has been restored to each and every one of you—however long it may take. So help me God."

Spontaneously, at the sound of cannon blasts, a variety of winged creatures left their nests to fill the night sky. A distinct fervor of renewed hope enraptured Lafitte as it did his men. Catherine had indeed been urging Jacques and his crew back to France. He was convinced of it.

4

Current Affairs

Charles never remarried. Impotent as he was, when Catherine entered his life, aside from her phenomenal attraction, his young bride's amusing fantasies generated a psychological aura that gave the King of France an arousal of ecstatic pleasure. Soon after Catherine's passing, Charles became melancholic, gave less heed to his royal duties, and shunned the proletariat's clamor for change.

For the exception of Monsieur Claude Truffaut, Charles's loyal valet, and Jacques Lafitte who, under duress, disclosed his secret to the Brotherhood of Dantes Revenge that Prince Louie had been fathered by their captain during a whirlwind interlude with the Queen, all France knew nothing of the Rose Garden incident. Though the king protected Louie from ambitious entrepreneurs attempting to gain favor and recognition while in the naive dauphin's presence, Charles's demeanor toward the young prince lacked the filial devotion a natural father would ordinarily bestow upon his offspring.

After Henry inherited the throne of England, he broke the treaty Edward, his predecessor, had made with France. French cargo vessels destined for the Netherlands and beyond were often waylaid by British galleons. The threat of war seemed imminent. Angry protestors once again gathered about the palace gates in droves demanding satisfaction for their neighbor's aggressive hostilities. Charles finally realized that by not confronting Henry head-on, the people of France viewed their king's actions of indifference as a sign of intolerable weakness.

Experiencing lapses of remorse over Catherine's death, Charles defaulted in concentrating on regal affairs. Aside from neglecting to monitor his cabinet ministers who misappropriated treasury funds for personal gain, he failed to oversee the various acquisition activities that had been ongoing in the Caribbean to ensure they were being properly conducted. In addition to all this, upon the announcement of an increase in taxes for the purpose of stemming the tide of imperial oppression, the bourgeoisie became incensed. Charles had to act swiftly or endure a reign of terror he cared not think about.

The King of France found himself facing yet another precarious dilemma. In the event of his unforeseen death, the fact remained Louie appeared to lack the inherent fundamental qualities necessary for a king to defend his throne from the very jackals who'd have the audacity to swear their allegiance to him. What's more, the young prince hadn't shown a keen desire to be King, or the slightest inkling in his demeanor to exact authoritative discipline on those he needed to control. The mere prospect of Louie being transformed into a puppet by any number of manipulative forces gave Charles grave concern.

Prince Louie had been cautioned many times not to be overly anxious about how the people would view him. He should always remember that not even a king could satisfy the wants of all his subjects. But what did it matter? He was still a child at heart. How could he perceive the haunting fate that awaited him in the not too distant future? Charles wondered how much time lingered in his own reign for him to outline and review, again and again, the essential steps Louie must adhere to, in safeguarding his succession to the throne from ending in total disillusionment.

It was about this time the *Sea Witch*, guised as a fishing vessel, snaked its way into Cherbourg's bustling harbor. Jacques Lafitte, relatively speaking, was only a stone's throw from embracing his son.

5

Cherbourg

Lafitte's first glimpses of Cherbourg, since he sailed to the Caribbean on Charles's five-mast ship, triggered intermittent flashes of his childhood days racing through his thoughts. Leticia, his mother, immediately came to mind. The harrowing episode, where she placed herself between a drunken sailor's bullet and her son, Jacques did not want to dwell upon it. While growing up under the tutelage of Dantes Lafitte, his intentions to visit her grave site never came to pass. Jaunts to Catherine's, Dantes's, and Leticia's places of interment were definite priorities on Jacques's forthcoming agenda. Lafitte didn't want to relive the past right now. To conjure up a way to embrace his son without revealing his secret (that Jacques Lafitte was indeed Prince Louie's birth father) would be the closest thing to holding Catherine in his arms.

The Port of Le Havre had been designated a temporary home base for Jacques Lafitte's elite crew. They'd find honest work and assist one another in trying to piece together how they would go about restoring whatever may still exist of their former lives. United in friendship and purpose, chains of fear and uncertainty no longer deterred them from claiming their rightful places in society. The consolation that Lafitte would assist them in their quest boosted the men's morale a hundredfold.

Malcolm de Salle, who aided Jacques in freeing several prisoners from the Bastille, volunteered to accompany Lafitte on his mission of being reunited with Louie. Having no family ties, de Salle considered it a personal honor to be his captain's humble servant in whatever capacity warranted his assistance. The plan was a simple one. After Jacques and Malcolm reconnoitered the prevailing situation, they'd establish a safe haven for the others to return to Paris. Somehow, they needed to find a way to restore themselves in the king's good favor.

Before parting their ways, Quicksand cautioned Lafitte. "Jacques, as much as you'd like to, for Catherine's honor and the boy's well-being, I need not remind you it'd be a fatal mistake if you were caught off guard in exposing your identity to anyone other than those whom you can trust. However, I'm inclined to believe the mangy beard, patched eye, and disheveled outfit you've chosen for a disguise could even fool me."

"You need not be overly concerned, Monsieur Peter La Ruche, for I doubt very much any of my former advocates are still in business."

"It's not your former enemies I'm worried about."

"Oh, you think Charles will see through me? Am I that transparent?"

"No, Jacques, it's that sensitive eye of yours. There's no telling how you'll react once you behold your son in the flesh."

Lafitte reflected for a moment on what Quicksand just said. With a wink and a smile, Jacques responded, "You're forgetting one thing, my friend."

"What's that?"

"You said it yourself. The one sensitive eye you've just alluded to will be covered up with a patch."

* * *

Jacques climbed aboard a carriage that would take him to Rouen, the first leg of his journey. Monsieur de Salle, his traveling companion, brought Lafitte up to snuff regarding the street news he learned while purchasing tickets for their trip to Paris.

As the coach bumped its way along the winding road, de Salle spoke concisely. "The air is filled with constant chatter of war. Thus far, neither France nor England has yet to make a formal declaration of breaking the peace. However Henry, within the past month, has sunk two more French cargo ships. What's more, Charles has not yet retaliated."

Lafitte responded, "I can never recall a time the King of France has ever recoiled from a fight. I wonder—that's one of the things I intend to find out."

"Perhaps Charles is stalling—for Louie's sake. His young prince, I mean, yours and Catherine's, must be prepared for the worst."

"Touché, Malcolm, it never occurred to me Charles may have taken an affinity to the boy. Soon, very soon, all the facts will be laid bare, and then—as Quicksand put it—action, not words, will be the order of the day."

6

Point of Contention

Catherine's prearranged marriage to Charles ultimately failed to unite England and France. Upon Edward's death, his arrogant son, Henry, charged that the King across the channel usurped his power by proclaiming rightful ownership to colonies in the Caribbean which had first been discovered by English explorers. Dialogue with Henry was useless. He refused to meet with Charles or enter into negotiations to settle his differences with France. For whatever reason, upset as he was, Henry tried to lure his neighbor into war. In the wake of a political debacle, the King of England, having probable cause, revved up hostilities between the two countries.

* * *

During an emergency conclave with his advisors, Charles vented his anger. "Those damn colonies, they'll be the death of me! Is there anyone among you who can produce a single shred of evidence Henry's allegations bear a semblance of truth, that France is responsible for seizing several of England's island possessions in the Caribbean?"

"Sire," it was Charles's Secretary Minister of Foreign Affairs, Monsieur Antoine Perot, who spoke up, "we've thoroughly investigated His Majesty Henry's strenuous protests. After researching the facts, there's reason to believe a few minor islands along the southern portion of the Lesser Antilles, having little consequential value, may have been first claimed by England's Admiral Burgess before our own Ambassador Colbert counterclaimed them for France. The time lines of these acquisitions allegedly, according to Sir Henry, had been fraudulently altered to appear France had lawful jurisdiction over them."

Perot nodded to a clerk who then unraveled a scroll and laid it before Charles. Antoine said, "The highlighted cluster of islands south of St. Vincent, as you can clearly see, are the ones in question. Also, farther to the northeast, just below the Bahamas, Sir Henry insists that the Caicos and Turks invariably belong to the Commonwealth of Great Britain."

Seated next to Perot, Stephan-Baptist Colbert appeared to be extraordinarily quiet. It was he who succeeded Governor Dupree soon after the statesman's assassination on the flagship, *Calcutta*. Stephan remained Chief Administrator of Colonial Affairs until he informed Charles just recently that it was necessary for him to resign his post due to health reasons. He'd been instrumental in procuring several Caribbean colonies that paradoxically had already been in the early stages of acquisition by other foreign imperialist nations, including England.

Amid an array of conflict and confusion, Colbert, finding himself in a position to do so, seized control of several colonies that had not been officially registered "departments" bearing the emblems of those sovereign nations that initially laid claim to them. Charles, never having been informed of what actually transpired, remained clueless as to why Henry persisted in his accusations that some of England's colonies had been illegally seized by France.

Colbert nervously reached for a glass of water. One of his unsteady fingers tipped the glass, spilling a portion of its contents. Attempting to divert Charles's attention from the matter at hand, he leaned back and barked, "Your Majesty, France is not prepared to engage in battle with a naval force stronger than her own. I suggest we placate Sir Henry, that is, for now. Perhaps it would be wise to appease the imperialist knave by surrendering to him that which he claims to be his. Later, at a time France regains its military strength, if it pleases you, my Lordship, we can reclaim that which is rightfully ours."

Charles stood up and paced the floor. One could hear a pin drop. He then paused and turned to look at his Minister of Colonial Affairs. In an enraged tone of voice he said, "Out with it, Colbert, for it was you and you alone who presided over the treaties in question. Whatever the truth, I want to hear it now. Concisely, what exactly is it you've been diligently keeping from your king all these years?"

Colbert choked. He surreptitiously glanced around to seek support from his colleagues. Finding none, Stephan-Baptist Colbert, without further ado, retrieved a miniature loaded pistol from his waistcoat and, holding it to his temple, pulled the trigger.

7

Lafitte's Agenda

As Lafitte's coach crossed into Rouen, a picturesque city on the Seine, flashbacks popped up of his and Dantes's several visits there during a time Jacques had seriously entertained the prospects of becoming a Roman Catholic priest. Graced with a variety of architectural splendor, the ancient Normandy city basked amid a natural flourish of rolling hills.

Before he and Malcolm reached Paris, it was essential for Lafitte to outline an agenda that would best accomplish his mission—to see, at all costs, Catherine's premonition of Louie's succession to the throne of France be a triumphant one. Lafitte realized, for this to come to pass, he needed to assume an assortment of roles that would assist his son in confronting whatever obstacles the young prince encountered once he became King.

After camping for the night at a roadside inn, de Salle suggested to Jacques they get plenty of rest before continuing on to Paris at daybreak.

"As you say, but first I want to review what we discussed earlier."

Malcolm withdrew a small notebook from his coat. Flipping to the first item on Lafitte's agenda, he read,

"*Trusted patriots:*

A. Monsieur Gilbert Montclair—Curio shop proprietor
B. Monsieur Bevier Lamont—Catherine's coachman
C. Monsieur Claude Truffaut—Charles's valet (?)

It's a rather short list. Why a question mark after Monsieur Truffaut?"

"Monsieur Truffaut is Charles's personal valet. He's the only one who can help me obtain vital pieces of information for which I need to put things into proper perspective. I'm wondering if his allegiance to the king may be such that he'll betray me once His Majesty's faithful servant learns my true identity."

"With the talk of war, I understand the palace gates are being heavily guarded. How will you even get close to Truffaut without being detected?"

"Perhaps I can devise a scheme whereby he and Monsieur Robert Murielle can rendezvous without raising any red flags."

"Who's Monsieur Murielle?"

"Monsieur Murielle, if you must know, is an aristocrat. How do you suppose I'll look impersonating an auditor? I've been in the business long enough to know that whenever there is a query made upon one's financial activities, nine times out of ten, the matter is attended to immediately."

"What if, after you reveal your true identity to him, Truffaut should decide to blow the whistle on you?"

"It's a chance I'll have to take, Malcolm. Somehow, I must convince Monsieur Truffaut that my purpose in returning to France is an honorable one. What's the next item on my agenda?"

"*Grave sites*"

"That's a personal matter I'll attend to in due course. Go on."

"*Secure adequate living quarters for our mates in Le Havre.* Jacques, I know a couple of halfway houses not far from the Bastille."

"I said adequate quarters. It's time dignity was restored in their lives."

"Good point."

"What's next?"

"*Disguises: Stable hand (Monsieur Ezra Giles)*—It looks as though your present outfit covers that one. *Solicitor (Monsieur Lambert Dubois)* is next on the list. Why will you need to impersonate a solicitor?"

"Quicksand can answer that. In any event, I may have to call upon you to assist me on this one." Before de Salle had time to question Lafitte as to what he meant by assisting him, Jacques emphatically said, "Next!"

"*Auditor (Monsieur Robert Murielle)*—We've already discussed and, last but not least, *Courier to Sir Henry (No name)*—You're really sticking your neck way out on this one."

"Let's get some sleep, Malcolm. We have a busy day ahead of us."

De Salle had made some salient points. Was Lafitte taking too much upon himself? Jacques pondered whether any of the elderly French patriots on his agenda were still alive. For Louie's sake, he hoped so.

8

Father and Son Talk

Louie, having heard the commotion that had just transpired in the conference room, observed Charles storming from the premises. Catching the king off guard, the young prince approached him and formally addressed his father as he had been instructed to do, "Your Majesty, all that noise in there, and that loud bang, it frightened me."

Charles, who had been noticeably shaken by what just transpired in the conference room, attempted to regain his composure. "Louie, must you go on being so fragile of spirit? Once I'm gone, France is going to need you to be strong."

"Don't talk like that, Sire, I've not yet gotten over my first fright. What will I do without you?"

Assuring Louie the ruckus he heard just now was nothing more than the usual bickering of officials displaying differences of opinion, he took the boy by the hand and said, "There's something I feel necessary you ought to hear. Don't worry, I'm not about to croak like a pigeon who lost its wings." Louie broke into a faint smile at Charles's words. "There, that's better. Come with me, Louie, let's take a stroll in the Rose Garden."

* * *

The Rose Garden, it was Charles's and Louie's favorite retreat. The king had often been asked by the prince child to describe what his mother was like. Never having gotten around to it, Charles said, "Louie, I shirked my duty in speaking of your mother at times you asked me to because it had been very difficult for me in choosing the precise words that would give proper insight into what she was really like."

Louie still hand in hand with Charles said, "I'm listening, Your Majesty."

"Even now, to describe your mother, I'm at a loss for words. However, I will try. Perhaps it's best that I put it this way. The next time you come across the sweetest looking rose in the garden, shall we start searching for it now? Single out among the others the one you consider to be the fairest."

Showing the way, Louie led Charles to a flowering rosebush that had recently been trimmed by one of the gardeners. "When at last you find it, smell of its fragrance and let the scent inebriate you. Be sure to ingest the contour of each supple leaf with a keen eye. Select one fragile petal and carefully, ever so carefully, run your finger along its tender surface."

Astonishingly, Louie paused, slowly disengaged Charles's hand from his own, and focused his eyes on a beige-colored rose whose elegant bloom stood out from the rest. Charles, noticing this, went on to say, "I promise you, my prince, sometime during the course of your meditative interlude, perhaps not at once, you will begin to inhale the mystifying secrets of your mother's heart and soul."

As Louie reached for the stem of the rose he'd been admiring, Charles's next words alerted the boy to pull back his hand. "Whatever you do, my youthful garçon, as much as you may be inclined, be not in haste to pluck it. For in doing so, your flower will not only die soon enough, but the reverie of your mother's admirable qualities too will quickly dissipate. You must be self-assured that once you've captured the essence of Catherine's loveliness, it will linger in your thoughts for as long as you choose to keep it alive."

It was then the two cradled each other's waist. With droplets of tears momentarily blurring his vision, Charles said, "I'm famished. Louie, what do you say we have our lunch on the veranda? Together, perhaps we'll be able to observe your mother's flower and secretly tell her from within our hearts how much we dearly love her."

9

Gilbert Revisited

After a tiresome journey, the outskirts of Paris loomed in sight. Lafitte wondered if he could pull it off. The task ahead seemed insurmountable. He and de Salle procured a room before setting forth to accomplish the various chores that had been included on today's agenda. Malcolm needed to establish suitable lodgings for the crew's return, while Jacques sought to look up an old friend. The mission had begun.

The exterior of Gilbert's Curio Shop looked much the same as Lafitte last remembered it. Glancing at the large display window next to the entranceway, Jacques instantly envisioned the prototype used as a model in the construction of the king's five-mast ship. However, when Lafitte entered the premises, it appeared as though the interior had been transformed into a thrift shop. All its former elegance and charm were nowhere to be seen. A gentleman, upon hearing the tinkling of the overhanging doorbell, appeared from behind a drawn curtain and approached his patron.

It was Gilbert. The years had noticeably taken a toll on him. Hunched over and walking with a limp in his stride, Montclair curiously peered at the vagabond who just entered his shop. "Good morning," he said, "how may I assist you?" Realizing the person before him was perhaps a penniless beggar, the shopkeeper quickly injected, "I was just about to have some tea. Would it interest you in joining me?"

Mortified, Jacques said, "Gilbert, it's me. Do you not recognize an old friend?"

"Step into the light so I can get a better look at you." What Gilbert said next was most heartwarming. "If I hadn't laid Monsieur Dantes Lafitte to rest with my own hands, I'd say you were he who'd come back from the resurrected life."

"Gilbert, my loyal friend, how long I've waited for this moment to thank you for the service you rendered to my father in my stead."

Speechless and unable to contain himself, Gilbert succumbed to tears. Embracing Monsieur Montclair, Lafitte said, "Forgive me, Gilbert, time is of the essence, and I can't explain everything to you now. What I'm praying you can do for me, my dear and noble friend, is to assist me in a matter of utmost urgency."

10

Ray of Sunshine

A ray of sunshine cast a beacon of light upon Lafitte. His hopes of seeing Louie for the first time, since he last held him in his arms on the *Dantes Revenge*, came much sooner than expected. Jacques learned from Gilbert that Agular, Pierre Fuquay's insidious henchman, trashed Monsieur Montclair's cameo shop. To show his gratitude in coming forth with pertinent information that enlightened the king to Pierre's deceitful charades, Charles engaged the proprietor in upgrading the palace interior with exquisite imported furnishings.

It happened to be the same time a string of handsome colts and mares arrived from England. They were a prideful gift from Catherine's father to her anticipated firstborn prince child. Shortly after Edward's sudden death, Catherine gave birth to Louie. Monsieur Bevier Lamont, commissioned by Charles, became the garçon's equestrian groom master. His task was to shape the future King into the finest horseman France had ever known.

Gilbert and Bevier became close associates. They saw to it that Louie had every conceivable amenity at his disposal. However, when France's economic state of affairs took a turn for the worse, the royal budget, being under close scrutiny, had to be stringently modified. Consequently, Gilbert's lucrative trade business came to a screeching halt.

Lafitte and his troupe could never have fled Paris without Monsieur Lamont's assistance. Knowing this, when Gilbert contacted Bevier informing him that Lafitte needed to gain admittance to the palace, in deference to Dantes Lafitte whom he considered one of France's finest statesmen, Catherine's faithful coachman made the entranceway to the stable gates accessible to Jacques.

* * *

Prince Louie had taken an immediate liking to Monsieur Ezra Giles (Jacques Lafitte) who was given the task of taking care of Sir York, the young dauphin's frisky horse. Surprisingly, when Jacques first spied his son, he did well to contain himself. His heart, however, was near bursting at the core with pride and sheer ecstasy.

Providentially, the new stable hand found an opportune moment to fulfill a dream come true. Sir York, spooked by a clap of thunder, reared the moment Louie climbed aboard. Lafitte, being in close proximity to the stallion, grabbed him by the reins, while at the same time cradled the young prince in his other arm before the lad hit the ground. "Whoa there, steady boy." Looking at the young garçon, Lafitte said, "Are you all right, Son?"

The prince quickly jerked his head around and looked at Giles. It was the first time anyone ever addressed him with that particular term of endearment. Seizing the moment, Lafitte did not wait for a response. He tenderly grasped Louie by the waist with both hands and gently hoisted him onto the saddle.

It was then Prince Louie said something out of the ordinary. Perhaps he was seeking affirmation or approval of some sort. "Monsieur Giles, do you think I'll make a good king one day?"

"Yes, my son, I think you'll make an admirable king." Lightheartedly, Giles added, "But it most assuredly will not be for just a single day. You will be the proud ruler of France for eons and eons. Why do you ask?"

Louie smiled at Monsieur Giles's facetious remark. He said, "Perhaps I shouldn't be sharing intimate secrets with someone I hardly know, but being you just saved me from a knock on the head, I recently put the same question to His Majesty."

Not once hearing an objection to being addressed "Son," Lafitte injected for a third time, "And what was his Lordship's response, my son?"

"He said it was too soon to tell, but if Mother were alive to have a say in the matter, I'd be a definite shoo-in." And with that, Louie gently kicked his heels and swiftly galloped away.

11

Bevier

During the two weeks that elapsed, while Monsieur Ezra Giles was establishing a close rapport with Louie who had taken an immediate liking to the new stable hand, Malcolm de Salle, at the request of his captain, set out for Le Havre to bring the crew of the *Sea Witch* back to Paris. It was then Lafitte surprised Bevier with unexpected news.

"Why must you leave so suddenly, Jacques? The young prince holds you in high esteem. How shall I explain your absence?"

"Tell my son, I mean Louie—"

"Jacques, you needn't have corrected yourself."

"Bevier, what are you implying?"

"From the very first moment I laid eyes on the garçon, I knew he was yours. You see, many years ago, at the time Lady Ann and King Henri were returning to Paris from Versailles, after an arduous climb to the top of a hill, we stopped to give the horses a breather. Quite by chance I overheard the King and Queen consoling one another. Apparently, the physicians at Centre Hospitalier de Versailles concurred that their son had inherited a rare birth defect that would impair Charles from ever bearing offspring."

Having been made aware of Charles's impediment prior to Catherine's death, Lafitte hesitated to say, "Isn't it quite possible Louie could have been sired by someone else?"

"Knowing full well you are trying to protect Louie from the calamity that is sure to ensue if, in fact, the truth of the matter became public knowledge, I forgive you, Jacques Lafitte, for what you just said."

Without furthering his pretentious attitude, Jacques yielded to Bevier's keen observation. "Who else knows about this, my intuitive friend?"

"To my knowledge, aside from Charles, only Monsieur Truffaut is aware of what we speak. Incidentally, as I understand, the physicians in question have long since taken their oath of silence about this to their final resting place."

Lafitte reflected for a few moments before saying, "Bevier, if I'm going to be Louie's protector in the throes of his perilous future, I can't rightly do it by confining myself to the palace stables. This is just one of many disguises I must use to fulfill Catherine's aspirations for her son. The time has come for me to make my presence felt."

Jacques then removed a chain from around his neck and said, "Give this to Louie. Tell the garçon Monsieur Giles wanted him to have it as a token of his affection for the prince. Try to make him understand I had to leave abruptly, that extenuating circumstances made it impossible for me to say good-bye. For now, he mustn't know the ring once belonged to Catherine's mother."

"What if Charles should recognize it?"

"I'm hoping he will. Sooner or later, we're bound to clash. Hopefully he'll have the common sense to realize I'm not a direct threat to revealing any of our secrets. Right now, I must get on with the business of making an appointment with Monsieur Claude Truffaut. Don't look so perplexed, my noble friend. Have faith. In the end, God's justice shall prevail."

It was then Bevier's turn to give Captain Lafitte a shot across the bow. He said, "Jacques, I'm not as confident in predicting God's ways as you seem to be. Monsieur Truffaut informed me only this morning, aside from his usual nightmares, Louie's troubles are just beginning. Claude assures me he has sufficient reason to believe the young prince is in mortal danger."

"Nightmares, mortal danger, Bevier, whatever else you've left unsaid, pray tell—keep not a word of it from me a moment longer."

12

Louie Interrupts

There was a faint knock on the king's chamber door. "Come in. What is it this time?" Without looking up from his escritoire, Charles said in an uneven, tempered voice, "Truffaut, haven't I forewarned you that I didn't want to be disturbed?" After a moment or two elapsed and the king didn't receive a response, Charles looked up and saw Louie standing by the door he had gently closed behind him.

"Oh, it's you. Louie, can't you see I'm very busy? These important matters of state must be attended to without delay. What is it you want?"

Drawing closer to Charles, the boy said hesitatingly. "I just wanted to converse with you, Father."

"How often has Truffaut instructed you to address me, Your Majesty?"

"Many times, Father."

Annoyed, Charles raised his voice. "There, you said it again."

"Said what, Father?"

"Not once, not twice, but thrice you have come in here and deliberately provoked me. Why?" Charles managed to contain himself. His anger somewhat softened.

Unafraid, Louie said, "I can understand addressing you with 'Yes, Your Highness, No, Your Majesty' as a matter of respect when we're on public display but . . ."

"So that's what you call it, public display. Never mind all this, now. What is it you wanted to speak to me about?"

"I guess it's not very important after all. I'm sorry to have disturbed you," and with a hint of sarcasm in his voice, Louie added, "Your Majesty."

"Come here, my prince." Getting up from his chair, Charles took the boy over to the window. He said, "Everything looks as it should. The gardens are in full bloom. Even the birds are in harmony today. The sun beats down upon the earth and gives it warmth and sustenance. I can go on and on, but it's my duty to inform you there is another side of the coin. You see, Louie, France has many adversaries, and the day will come soon enough when she'll depend upon your mighty sword to defend her crown. The best intentions of a king can only be measured by the caliber of strength he wields against those who'd dare oppose him. That's all your mother would have wanted, Louie, for you to be noble and strong."

Moving closer to Charles, Louie said, "I just want us to be Father and Son. Isn't that what Mother would have wanted?"

Charles, taken aback, said, "Perhaps I've been somewhat remiss. From now on, I'll make it a point to spend more quality time with the future King of France. There's much for you to learn, and who better to teach you than I?"

Noticing a blank stare on Louie's face, Charles facetiously added, "Now, young man, if I don't get back to work, the people of France will think I've gone soft in dealing with your blithering uncle across the channel."

Not saying anything, Louie affirmatively nodded his head. As he abruptly turned to exit, the decorative bells on his princely garment jingled softly. Charles asked, "Is there anything in particular that prompted you to see me just now?"

"It's only that Monsieur Giles once slipped with his tongue and called me Son. I thought if he could address me, Son, I certainly should be able to address you Father."

With a wink in his eye, Charles said, "Why, I'll give that fellow ten whips of the lash myself. Who does the rascal think he is calling the dauphin to the throne of France his Son?"

The king noticed a trinket dangling from a silver chain that looked strangely familiar. When asked how he came by it, Louie thought it best just to say an admirer gave it to him.

Anxious to get on to more important matters, Charles (not recognizing Catherine's ring) said, "Louie, my son"—it was the first time he called him that—"once you become King, you'll be inundated with many trinkets whose sources of origin will soon become a distant memory. Now off with you, my prince, I have work to do."

Before leaving, Louie said, "Incidentally, Father, you won't have any need to give Monsieur Giles ten flogs of your lash."

The king's voice remained unperturbed when he said, "Isn't that for me to decide?"

"I'm not questioning your authority, Your Majesty. It's just that no sooner had Monsieur Giles arrived at the stables, he's already left us."

13

Monsieur Murielle

Lafitte intercepted Claude Truffaut before he entered le Banc de Paris. Flashing his credentials, Jacques said, "Monsieur Truffaut I take it—my card."

"My account is in perfectly good standing. Monsieur Murielle, I must forewarn you, if the accusatory remarks cited in the message I received by your firm requiring me to meet you here are not resolved in a timely manner to my satisfaction, the king shall hear of this."

"My carriage is waiting to take us to le Café Emerald. It's the least I can do to make amends for the unfortunate error which has been assessed to your account. Due to a clerical oversight, it was inadvertently taken for someone else's. You see the serial numbers are nearly identical to one another for the exception of one digit. Please accept my humble apologies for any embarrassment this may have caused you."

"Very well, monsieur, even I upon a rare occasion can make a mistake. Thank you for your reconciliatory offer. I assure you, it is quite unnecessary. Good day."

"But it is necessary. There's a far more pressing issue we must discuss than the meeting of the minds over a mere ten thousand francs overdraft."

"Kindly enlighten me, Monsieur Murielle, precisely what is it you're talking about?"

"Not here, Monsieur Truffaut, not here. What I have to say is of the utmost importance. Perhaps the future welfare of all France may very well be in your hands."

"In my, my hands, you say?"

"Shall I explain everything while we dine? Come, my good man, our carriage awaits us."

14

Communiqué

The law of succession to the throne of France, upon extinction of direct male descendents to the king, would then laterally pass to Charles's only sibling, Prince Philippe who resided in Fontainebleau Castle. The palace was more like a fortress. Its impenetrably high walls were complemented by a deep moat that encircled the citadel. Louie's birth had become an immediate threat to his uncle's aspirations of being next in line to inherit the crown. Charles, totally aware of Philippe's insatiable desire to be King, forbade him to reside in Paris.

Nearly a year had passed since the two brothers had communicated with one another. However, the customary ritual of Philippe's attendance at Charles's coronation anniversary was drawing nigh. Fearful that he might find an opportune moment to place Louie in harm's way, Charles would confine his son to a cloistered segment of the palace under a twenty-four-hour guard until his ambitious brother's visit had expired.

However, two months before the annual event was to be celebrated, Charles received a communiqué from one of his undercover agents stationed in Fontainebleau that Philippe intended to secretly rendezvous with the King of England within a fortnight's time. This could mean only one thing: a treasonous plot to usurp the throne of France had already been set in motion. As much as Charles detested his brother, it grieved him to think that the only plausible solution in resolving the imminent coup d'état was to assassinate the Prince of Fontainebleau before he met with Henry.

15

Truffaut's First Revelation

Taking a sip of wine, Truffaut delicately placed his beveled glass on the table reserved for exclusive patrons wishing to remain obscured from public view. The gaudy crimson curtains cordoning off the cubicle were practically soundproof. He said, "Monsieur Lafitte, I commend you for exercising good judgment in keeping your true identity secretive. Monsieur Lamont and I are most vigilant wherein Prince Louie is concerned and, I might add, the king as well. However, with all that has transpired of late, I'm inclined to believe your return to Paris may very well be a godsend."

"Claude, just before I left my situation at the stables, Monsieur Lamont told me Louie is deeply troubled by frightful dreams and that his life might be in grave danger."

"Concisely, I can tell you only what I've heard. Louie frequently hallucinates in his sleep. His dreams rarely differ. Apparently, the boy's mother, whose facial features are blurred in a cloud of white mist, seems to be reaching out to him. She is alone and tied to the mast of a foundering ship. Louie, in attempting to save her, is confronted with ghastly sea creatures much too horrible to describe."

Lafitte remained dumbfounded while Truffaut continued speaking, "Charles has been working very diligently in painting a calm, serene picture of Catherine. Words of reassurance that the Queen of France is quite safe living among a host of God's precious angels have indeed helped to suave the garçon's woeful thoughts. However, the king's personal physician believes the young prince may have captured at birth a mirage of his mother's inner struggle, which thus far he has been unable to disentangle from his recurring night dreams."

"Truffaut, while masquerading as Monsieur Ezra Giles, Louie and I were just beginning to strike up a trusting relationship. There are many facets of Catherine's character he ought to know about. Perhaps, if I—"

Anticipating what Jacques was about to say, Truffaut interrupted him with, "No, Monsieur Lafitte, the prince must never know you are his true father. Any intimacy you shared with his mother, however pure and innocent it may have been, must not come to light at this time. There's no telling what the shock would do to him. Worse than that, aside from Charles, all France would be embroiled in turmoil."

"Trust me, Truffaut, as difficult it is for me to say, divulging my identity to Louie is regrettably the one thing I can never do. However, more importantly, not to minimize anything we've already discussed, apprise me of the mortal danger Bevier has alluded to that is presently hovering over my . . ." Realizing he needed to refrain from imaging Louie as his son, Lafitte instead said, "Prince Louie. Then, afterward, I'd very much appreciate it if you would be so kind to enlighten me as to where Catherine has been interred."

16

Charles's Ultimatum

Charles, realizing he had to act swiftly, called for an emergency cabinet meeting. He regarded Stephan-Baptist Colbert's suicide an admission of guilt for inappropriate behavior befitting a royal minister to the king. Henry's vehement protests, that several of England's colonial claims were fraudulently repossessed by France during an intermittent blackout timeline period, needed to be addressed.

More importantly, however, it was a prime concern that something conclusive had to be done about Prince Philippe. If Charles did not maintain sovereign control over the downward spiraling situation, his reign was certainly to end in a cataclysmic revolt. In all probability, Philippe, inveigling a way to rid himself of Louie, would then ascend the throne of France as Henry's puppet.

"Gentlemen, in the event the two issues at hand are not satisfactorily resolved, I assure you this conclave will terminate with several immediate beheadings, all of which are currently resting on your shoulders." Gasps of indignation reverberated throughout the room.

Ignoring the committee's spontaneous reaction to his display of morbid humor, Charles retorted in a resolute voice, "Yea or nay, do we surrender the colonies in question to Sir Henry, or do we go to war with England? I also want your candid opinion as to whether the treasonous Prince of Fontainebleau, my devious, ambitious brother, should live or die."

Charles sat back and said, "Councilmen, for now I'll say no more. Consult with one another. Consider most diligently the matters I've set before you. Hopefully, before the hour expires, this elite body will have come up with a viable solution that'll save your king the embarrassment of having to engage France in a senseless bloodbath."

17

Truffaut's Final Revelation

While their food grew cold, Truffaut explained to Lafitte that Charles's brother posed a definite threat to Louie's ascension to the throne. "The last thing I learned before leaving the palace," he said, "there's talk Philippe intends to rendezvous with Sir Henry quite soon. Even as we speak, Charles is meeting with his administrators to review the matter. He's hoping they'll provide a solution to this dilemma. In any case, I believe His Majesty is not in a position to prevent Philippe from shuffling off to England. As it is, Charles has barely enough loyal gendarmes to safeguard the palace."

"So this is the mortal danger Monsieur Lamont made reference to the other day."

"Philippe will stop at nothing to secure the throne of France. I cannot bring myself to express the exact words, but yes, His Majesty and Prince Louie's lives are in perilous danger."

"Truffaut, we haven't much time to discuss all that's going through my mind. You must arrange for me an audience with Charles. I've got to talk to him soon, very soon."

"You can't be serious. In his present state of mind, he'll have you guillotined before reflecting upon what he's doing. And I might add, he'll do the same to me as well for conspiring with you."

"Charles will not have to know we collaborated. I've already found a suitable disguise that will secure my admittance to the palace without being recognized. I believe, after Charles listens to all I have to say, he will no longer consider his brother a threat to either Louie or the throne of France."

"Whatever will you tell him?"

"In good time, my good man, in good time. But right now, I must know where Catherine has been interred."

Sworn to secrecy regarding this matter, Truffaut could not find it within himself to betray Charles. He said, "Why it's common knowledge the Queen of France is entombed in the royal quadrant of Saint Monica's Cemetery. Why do you ask?"

Lafitte spoke in a melancholic tone of voice when he said, "I visited her there just yesterday. I'm certain it was the right place. The mausoleum was adorned with freshly cut flowers. Everything appeared as it should, peaceful and quiet. However, I felt a distinct chill in the air. It was as though Catherine's corpse had vanished from the grave site. Tell me, Truffaut, I must know. Where is she?"

Shaken to his senses that the absence of the queen's remains could only have been revealed to Lafitte by powers higher than a King's authority, Truffaut reluctantly said, "Catherine rests tranquilly among the flowers in the palace's Rose Garden. I'm inclined to believe it will not be necessary for me to show you the precise location."

"Undisturbed, is she, if only it were true? The one thing Catherine prized more than anything was her tiara. Knowing her crown was encased in one of the stolen treasure chests, it had been the solitary reason why I took up the search, hoping I'd find it—to one day return it to her final resting place."

"Be most assured as we speak, Catherine wears the tiara Charles had presented to her upon the day of their betrothals."

"It's common knowledge the Queen's wedding gift from the king was looted during the storm at sea."

"Not so, Charles never sent it off in the treasure chest. He had cleverly distracted the entire assemblage, including Monsieur Fuquay, during which time he removed Catherine's crown from the casket and switched it with an identical facsimile before it was sealed. The king intended to surprise her, but his Queen sailed off to the Caribbean instead to find you, which I'm now convinced she considered to be her ultimate prized possession."

Jacques paused for a moment and then said, "Of course, Charles had Catherine interred in the Rose Garden, so he could be ever close to her."

It was then Truffaut divulged yet another volley of bad news. "You may as well hear it sooner than later, Monsieur Lafitte. Charles's physicians believe the King of France's health is failing. And this is why you must be extremely cautious in how you intend to approach him. If the tenuous situation at hand or his uncontrollable tantrums do not do him in, then perhaps it will be the shock of your sudden reappearance that will precipitate his final demise."

"For Louie's sake, let's hope Charles grants me the few moments I need to assure him that I've returned to France to be of service, not to hinder."

18

Reunion

Upon Malcolm de Salle's arrival in Le Havre, the *Sea Witch's* crew became overjoyed. "Mates," he said, "we'll sail to Versailles at the next incoming tide, and from there, leave by coach to Paris. Thanks to Monsieur Lambert Dubois, I have papers for all of you."

Quicksand inquisitively asked, "Malcolm, who's Monsieur Dubois, is he one of Lafitte's former comrades?"

"No, my curious friend, he *is* Lafitte. Never mind that now, I'll explain everything while we voyage homeward.

* * *

Jacques Lafitte brought his crew up to speed on recent developments. There was much to do and very little time in which to do it. His foremost concern was Prince Louie whose life was proven to be in grave danger. Although a few of Jacques's men still had to address unresolved personal matters, for Lafitte to implement a tactful plan of action in carrying out his mission, he needed the full complement of his dedicated corsairs securely placed within the palace walls.

It was difficult to assume that Charles, being exceedingly cautious, would be inclined to receive a stranger seeking an audience with him. However, if Lafitte presented himself in disguise as a special emissary bearing news from Sir Henry, Charles—having to be kept duly informed of the devious king's latest proposals—had little choice but to precipitously acknowledge the English courier's presence.

It was then three coaches pulled up to the rented cottage. "Who could that be?" Muslim Green inquired with a whisper.

Entering the shelter, Malcolm de Salle said, "I'm sorry we're late, but I had to be sure we weren't being followed. Gentlemen, I'm honored to present to you Monsieur Gilbert Montclair. He's brought each of you newly tailored uniforms that must be donned without delay." Looking at Lafitte, Malcolm added, "Don't you agree, Jacques, that these honorable former inmates of the Bastille will make a splendid addition to His Majesty's royal guard?"

Lafitte said in response, "That, Malcolm, goes without saying, however, I suspect Monsieur Truffaut is anxiously anticipating our arrival within the hour. The matter concerning a deed that needs to be restored to its rightful owner will have to wait."

Mystified, Quicksand said, "We, fugitives of the king, Swiss Guards, property being restored? Whose property?"

"Your property, Monsieur La Ruche, the very same inheritance Pierre Fuquay deviously awarded to your conniving stepbrother. You and Malcolm will soon pay Monsieur Blanchford a visit, who, I might add, found it in his best interest to change his name. With you having been sentenced to the Bastille, the mere mention of the surname, La Ruche, had suddenly become an embarrassment to personages seeking higher nobility.

"Be not overly concerned about this, Quicksand, Monsieur Blanchford will soon be more than happy to revoke his claim to your estate."

"But how?"

"By making the scheming rascal an offer he cannot refuse. In any event, your soon-to-be reinstated inheritance may very well be needed to procure a safe haven for Prince Louie, which reminds me, it's time for me to don my ingenious disguise."

De Salle said, "I've already prepared your costume. It's hanging up in your boudoir."

Lafitte looked at everyone and said, "Gentlemen, I'll explain everything just before we leave for the palace. Malcolm, Monsieur Montclair will assist you in getting the men ready. Come now, we haven't a moment to lose. France's future depends upon our success. I'm certain of it."

19

Items of Concern

While his ministers attempted to sort out the king's mandates, Charles soon became impatient in listening to their constant bickering. It was then Dr. Jonathan Clifford entered the chamber and whispered in His Majesty's ear. Charles abruptly stood up and said, "Gentlemen, a matter of urgency necessitates my brief absence. However, upon my return, I expect this council to lay before me a plan of action that will satisfactorily resolve the precarious situation in which we find ourselves."

The senate members, fearful of Charles, needed to exercise extreme precaution in coming to terms with the king's two sanctions—how to deal with Sir Henry and what to do with Prince Philippe. Each minister realized it would be fatal to voice an opinion contrary to what they believed Charles wanted to hear. The slightest leaning toward ambivalence, passivity, compromise, divisiveness, or surrender would most certainly precipitate His Majesty's ire.

No sooner than Charles had left the room, Monsieur Antoine Perot, Secretary Minister of Foreign Affairs, rose to his feet and said, "Colleagues, it will be a detriment to France if we concede to King Henry's demands. As for Prince Philippe, who among you has the audacity to tell His Lordship upon his return that the council unanimously proposes that his brother must die?"

* * *

Charles gently patted Prince Louie's forehead. Without looking at the physician he said, "How long has he been uttering these latest incoherencies?"

"The prince had a rather prolonged ride today. He was napping only for a short time before he commenced to call out to his mother. Naturally, I reported the matter to you immediately."

"Is there anything else?"

"No, Your Majesty, we've done all that is conceivably possible. I would only suggest that you continue to reassure the young prince, at such times he awakens from his deliriums, that the Queen of France is resting quite peacefully and is completely impervious to the tortures maligning his dreams." Charles nodded affirmatively and left Louie's bedside. Of all his regal problems, his prince's frightful nightmares were the most difficult for him to bear.

While retreating to his private quarters to seek a moment's rest, Charles was met by yet another messenger. Recognizing the seal on the envelope, he hesitated for a brief moment before breaking it. The dispatch came from an independent Swiss company established by neutral European countries to arbitrarily assess and record official documents pertaining to all

Caribbean "departmental settlements" dating back to Christopher Columbus's first discoveries. Upon reading the communiqué he had been long awaiting, Charles had very little choice but to act as he must.

20

Veil of Deceit

Philippe's Lieutenant general, Anton Chambier, had seen to it that the precise time of his prince's departure from France remained a guarded secret. The inconspicuous entourage was to snake its way through sparsely populated areas until it reached the northern breakwaters of Tourcoing which overlooked the English Channel. From there, Charles's brother was to sail northwest where Sir Henry agreed to meet with him at Dover Castle.

The two conspiring monarchs, whose paths had never crossed, needed to finalize the terms of a pact designed to ultimately bring the King of France's incumbency to a devastating conclusion. By means of military assistance provided by King Henry, upon Philippe's seizing control of France, the Prince of Fontainebleau would then ingratiate England with two additional Caribbean settlements, aside from the ones currently being disputed.

After Charles was officially ousted from the throne, it had also been conceded that English merchant vessels would be granted immunity from paying all excise revenues while trading with France. However, before any of this came to fruition, Charles's ambitious brother had to demonstrate a rightful claim to be the king's legitimate successor. Hence, Prince Louie's end of days were nigh upon him.

Shortly before Prince Philippe's departure for England, one of the king's adept informers, Mademoiselle Lissette Van dermal, during a lascivious interlude with Chambier, cajoled from her pretentious lover the sordid details of Philippe's treasonous intentions. Charles, realizing the necessity to share Van dermal's telltale dispatch with his cabinet ministers, made an about-face and headed for the conference room. It was during this time Jacques Lafitte, accompanied by a platoon of his men masquerading as Swiss Guards, sought entrance to the palace.

"Monsieur," he said to the gatekeeper, "I have an urgent message for His Highness, King Charles of France."

Following explicit instructions, the sentry said, "Pardon, but His Worship is not receiving visitors at this time."

Monsieur Claude Truffaut, expecting the contingent's prearranged arrival, intervened and said to the Sergeant at arms, "Let them enter. His Majesty is most eager to have an immediate audience with our English visitors."

Turning to Lafitte, Truffaut added, "Welcome to France, I trust you had a pleasant journey. Gentlemen, this way please."

21

Unexpected Visitor

Moments before the King of France reentered the antechamber, Claude Truffaut came rushing up to him and said, "Your Grace, I've just been informed that a courier from England has an urgent message that requires your immediate attention."

"Do you suppose it's another bulletin from Sir Henry suggesting I relinquish, aside from the colonies he's already proclaimed to be his, half of France as well?"

"Most unlikely, Your Majesty, this way, if you please."

* * *

When Charles entered the visitor's parlor, Lafitte's back had been turned toward him. It appeared the English courier had the impudence to engage in an informal conversation with the king's own guard. Charles facetiously said, "The next time Sir Henry has a dispatch for me, kindly inform His Lordship to deliver it by way of carrier pigeon."

Upon his turning about, Charles recognized Jacques Lafitte immediately. "Seize this man," he barked angrily to the gendarmes.

"They're with me," Lafitte's response was casual.

"Truffaut, what is the meaning of this preposterous outrage?"

"Your Majesty, forgive me for this apparent deception, but it was the only means of arranging your meeting with Monsieur Lafitte. Accurately forecasting your spontaneous reaction upon seeing him, he's asked me to assure you that he's come to speak to Your Grace in friendship and that whatever differences may linger between you they must be held in abeyance until you have heard him out."

Before Charles had a chance to speak, Truffaut said to Lafitte's corsairs, "Gentlemen, this way, if you please?" The king's servant knew he had taken a chance. If Jacques was unable to convince Charles that his mission was fraught with good intentions, His Liege whom he served since the day of his coronation, would look upon him as a worthless traitor. Although Charles did hold his tongue, it was his glaring look that gave Claude Truffaut sufficient reason to exhibit an obvious twitch in his gait.

22

Plot to Kill

In the process of refilling Chambier's goblet, Prince Philippe said, "I'm planning to leave for England a day or two ahead of schedule. There are several sensitive issues I need to discuss with Sir Henry, especially my guaranteed protection, in the event an unforeseen revolt occurs after Charles and Louie are dispensed with. In my absence, you're quite sure everything will be carried out according to plan?"

"Barring unforeseen circumstances, Your Eminence, in less than ten days you will be proclaimed by order of your birthright the next King of France."

"To think, during which time I'm mending broken fences with Charles's dubious archenemy, I can hardly be suspected of having anything to do with the contrivances of my poor brother's assassination. Anton, I have complete confidence that your cleverly devised scheme cannot fail. Reiterate, if you will, the sordid details one last time so I can relish the event, as though I were there to witness it myself."

"As you wish, my Liege. Eight days from now, Charles will make his annual visitation to Saint Monica's Cemetery for a brief visit to Catherine's mausoleum. As you know, he's upheld this tradition most faithfully. Your brother and nephew will depart from their carriage to place a wreath of roses alongside the queen's tomb. At the precise moment they kneel to humble themselves before the throng of onlookers, Lord Charles will be slain by a two-edged sword that one of the disguised monks in the ecclesiastical entourage has concealed within the folds of his habit. Ten seasoned archers will then focus their arrows on Louie. They all cannot miss. After the mass confusion is over, everyone will naturally think their precious prince unavoidably became an innocent victim in the assassination plot against the king."

Chambier gulped down a swallow of nectar from his chalice and continued to say, "A contingent of your loyal cavaliers, impersonating the king's guard, whose actions would hardly be questioned by bewildered spectators, will then proceed to whisk the perpetrator away in great haste. Before any of the mourners fully realizes what had just occurred, those associated with Charles's and Louie's deaths shall have left the grounds either by coach or by horseback."

"And I will receive a dispatch of this dastardly deed while I'm still in England?"

"It's already been drafted, Your Grace. Shall I read it to you verbatim?"

"No, Anton, I wish for my reaction to its contents be one of genuine surprise. Perhaps the shocking news will enable me to shed a tear or two. In any event, no one, excepting Henry of course, could possibly affirm that my tears, if they should spontaneously occur, will have been initiated by sheer joy."

Consciously feeling his importance in the scheme of things, Anton said, "I solemnly vow, Your Grace, Louie will never be coronated King of France, not so long as I shall live."

Raising his goblet, Philippe proposed a toast, "Long life to you, my faithful servant, and a very long life indeed."

23

Charles and Lafitte

Part I

The instant Truffaut left the antechamber with Lafitte's men who had been posing as centurions of the Swiss Guard, Charles went into a tirade. "How dare you return to France after I explicitly commanded you not to exceed the borders of French soil until the sovereign treasures have been fully recovered?"

Retrieving the *Sea Witch's* logbook from his coat, Jacques tossed it on the table and shot back, "For sixteen insufferable years, my crew and I aimlessly searched the high seas, and for what? No, Your Majesty, rather permit me the privilege to tell *you* why. Charles, you never cared an iota as to what became of the treasure. Is the entire world to believe that an enormous wealth of riches was to embark on such an arduous voyage without first being adequately insured by its respective heads of state?"

"Do not be so naive, Monsieur Lafitte, you've somehow conveniently managed to discount the numerous precious items that were among the irreplaceable stolen jewels. However, I suspect you already know this."

"Catherine's tiara undoubtedly ranks among them?"

Charles glared at Lafitte. Had Catherine mentioned to him she believed her coronet had been encased among the treasures? He calmly said, "What concern of this is yours?"

"Why didn't you tell her, Charles? She may be alive today if only you had told her the truth."

"So Truffaut has deemed it necessary to betray his trust in this as well? What else has he told you?"

"Since you asked, I learned that Louie is beset with nightmarish dreams. It's beyond comprehension, the way Truffaut described them to be."

"What other royal secrets has Monsieur Truffaut so ordained to escape from His Majesty's Pandora's box?"

"He's confided in me that you are extremely ill. Before he permitted me to see Your Grace, I had to give him my solemn word to remain unruffled in spite of your unpredictable temperament."

"How considerate of him—to think I've implicitly placed my unconditional trust in Claude all these years."

"Perhaps it may be difficult for you to understand, Your Majesty, but it was exclusively after convincing Monsieur Truffaut I returned to France with the utmost honorable intentions of serving my king, he discharged from his troubled soul only that which he considered necessary for me to know. In truth what I have come to say may not be altogether agreeable, however, I'm certain that if you receive my words with an open heart, they will serve you well"

Surprisingly, Charles reverted his training of thought to a previous exchange of words. He said to Lafitte in a subdued voice,

"I did intend to tell Catherine that I discreetly withdrew her tiara from the casket of Crown jewels, but not before the treasure ships weighed anchor. I wanted to see the ecstatic surprise in Catherine's crestfallen spirit when I presented it to her later that evening. Distraught as she was, it never once occurred to me my beloved queen would go through such extraordinary lengths to pursue her most prized possession to the far corners of the earth."

"Charles, then you truly do not believe Catherine stowed away in hopes of finding me?"

"The concept did cross my mind, but no, Catherine under any circumstances would not have deserted me. As a woman obsessed by inexplicable fantasies, she'd have been contented enough just being the mother to your child. However, if Catherine were alive today, as Queen of France, the two of us would proceed about our royal business without the necessity of having to endure any additional interference from you. So help me God, let it not have been otherwise."

It was then, while totally engrossed in a book of verses, Prince Louie suddenly opened the door and entered the room.

24

Charles and Lafitte

Part II

Upon noticing Charles conversing with a visitor, Prince Louie said, "Pardon me for the interruption, Father, but I thought you might like to know I'm feeling much better now."

"Come, let me embrace you, my son. It's good to see you are looking your usual self."

Placing the book of verses he held in his hand on a nearby settee, Louie went over to Charles and submitted to his comforting arms of endearment.

Jacques Lafitte was spontaneous to speak. "You must be Prince Louie. It's indeed an honor to have at last seen you up close."

"I'm honored to meet you as well, Monsieur . . ."

"Monsieur Lambert Dubois," Lafitte quickly injected.

Spying Lafitte somewhat curiously, Louie said, "Have I not seen you somewhere before?"

"Monsieur Dubois has recently returned from the Caribbean, Louie. We've much to discuss before he returns to . . ." Charles hesitated.

"Martinique, Your Majesty, it's evolving into one of your most promising colonial acquisitions."

"Martinique, why, Father, isn't that where Mother was voyaging to before she—" Louie abruptly cut short what he was about to say. Turning toward Lafitte, he said, "Sir, did you by any chance know my mother?"

Charles remained speechless.

Lafitte said, "Yes, my prince, you see, while the queen was in the midst of her adventurous journey, she wished to learn specifically how the heavens served as a compass in guiding seafaring vessels to their perspective destinations. I was privileged to be the navigator on your mother's ship and assisted her to understand some of the various nautical terms employed in a seaman's manual."

"Louie," Charles interrupted, "will you be so kind to tell Monsieur Truffaut to inform the members of my council that I will be rejoining them momentarily?"

"Certainly, Father." Turning to Lafitte, the prince said, "It's been a pleasure to have met your acquaintance, Monsieur Dubois. Perhaps, upon my return, you wouldn't mind sharing some pertinent details of Mother's adventures with Father and me."

Slightly bowing his head toward Louie, Lafitte said, "Adieu, my prince, I can think of no higher honor."

25

Charles and Lafitte

Part III

After Prince Louie left the room, Charles's temper flared. He said to Lafitte, "I'm curious to know how you managed to easily convince Truffaut that you returned to France by simply implying to him that you had the utmost honorable intentions of serving your king. He's not so naive as he pretends to be. What exactly is it you told him that he dared to betray every one of our confidences?"

Lafitte proceeded to shout back, "Not every confidence, Charles, just the ones he felt compelled to divulge. You see, Your Majesty, I assured Truffaut that I'd rather lay down my life before ever considering to claim Louie to be my own. One of the last things Catherine asked of me was to promise that nothing stood in Louie's way of becoming one of France's most proud and noblest rulers."

Charles retaliated, "Do you mean to tell me I'm aloof, that I'd allow Louie to be surrounded by incompetent fools?"

"From the very day you became King, you entrusted the administration of your kingdom to ambitious imbeciles who have wrought much shame and dishonor upon the people of France."

"How dare you be so contemptible? If my memory serves me correctly, you and your father held key positions in my cabinet. Are you insinuating Dantes Lafitte was a villainous traitor?"

"Leave him out of this. If you recall, it was His Majesty, Henri, your father, may he rest in peace, who had appointed Dantes long before you ascended the throne. It was because of Dantes and the likes of your former Minister of Foreign Affairs, Governor Jean Dupree, France was able to gain a stronghold in the West." Lafitte continued with a hint of abashment in his voice, "As for me, it's true. I've wronged you without saying and have much to answer for."

"Finally, you admit to your shame. Does it now give you the audacity to storm my palace to seize control of your son?"

"Louie is not my son, not if he is to be the next King of France."

"What are you saying?"

"Charles, come to your senses. I have not returned to France for the purpose of laying claim to Louie. It was Catherine who insisted that I see that no harm comes to him. From what I learned from Truffaut, the boy may be in grave danger."

"So he's also informed you of my brother's ardent desire to succeed me to the throne of France. I'm well aware of the situation. Like you, Philippe's not immune to the guillotine."

"That's all France needs right now, a blood war among its reigning monarchs."

"You do think me a fool. Hear me well, Lafitte, my beloved brother, Prince Philippe, has already set in motion a plot to assassinate both his king and Louie."

"Charles, listen to me. Time is of the essence. I ask only this of you—hear me out. If, after what I have to say does not go well with you, I will break my promise to Catherine and abide by your wishes."

"And if I reject your proposal, what then?"

"For the manner in which I have grieved Your Majesty in the past, should it amuse my king to do so, you may have my head on a platter."

26

Charles and Lafitte

Part IV

While Charles patiently waited for Lafitte to bare his soul, Jacques paced the floor, wondering where to begin. Spying Louie's book of verses on the bench, he went over to it and said, "Your Majesty, nothing has inspired me more, in spite of how you feel about me personally, than to see the remarkable intimacy that you and Louie share with one another."

"Louie is Catherine's son. He means everything to me. Is there a relevant point to this particular observation?"

"Just a few moments ago, the young prince appeared quite interested in learning of his mother's adventures on the high seas."

"It seems only natural that he makes such inquires."

"Charles, do you think it will be beneficial to Louie if I were to describe to him in explicit detail how wonderfully his mother behaved in the face of extreme danger?"

"I honestly doubt it would make a difference. Be as it may, I believe Louie inherited from Catherine whatever trauma she had been experiencing before she entered her comatose condition. The most skilled physicians believe his dreams will continue to plague him until . . ."

"Charles, I'm not so presumptuous as to consider myself a healing specialist, and as you say, Louie may never recover from his ill-fated dreams, but I've thought of something that might truly venture beyond the usually prescribed cure-alls."

"You'd like to take him on a voyage, wouldn't you, Monsieur Lafitte?"

"Charles, your clairvoyance amazes me. Yes, Your Highness, the thought did cross my mind."

"Has it now? That which you propose is out of the question. You see, Louie is in grave danger." Removing a packet of ribbon-bound letters from his escritoire, Charles continued to say, "Every one of them is identical—*The Prince of Fontainebleau will be next in line to inherit the Throne of France.*"

Jacques Lafitte was persistent. "Charles, right now, the palace is vulnerable and subject to being attacked. Until it's safe for Louie to be moved to a temporary location which will keep him out of harm's way, my men will maintain a constant vigil over him. You must consider your own personal safety as well."

In the midst of curtailing his fury, Charles said, "And you expect me to adhere to your preposterous overtures as though the gates to my fortress were freely left unguarded?"

"Allow me, if I may, to speak directly."

"Though it will be a waste of time, and other important matters are awaiting my presence this very moment, please do."

Lafitte spoke compellingly. "Charles, the soldiers that accompanied me here are my trusted shipmates. They're dedicated to Your Majesty's service. All they ask of you is to be reinstated to their former ranks of citizenship, which they rightfully inherited before Pierre Fuquay twisted the letter of the law to take it from them."

Lafitte's next words had taken Charles by surprise. "Your Grace," he said, "how easy it was for my mates and me to get so close to Louie. What if, by chance, we happened to have been a contingent of Prince Philippe's elite guard?"

Without warning, the king suddenly buckled. While stretching his arms toward Lafitte, Charles held on to him for support. The king instinctively retrieved a vial from his garment, uncorked it, and quickly swallowed the elixir. It took only a matter of seconds before he began to recover from his seizure. "Jacques," he said to Lafitte's total disbelief, "where exactly will you be taking Louie?"

"When it's safe, my men will take him to a nearby haven, which you yourself will provide." Withdrawing an envelope from his courier's satchel, Jacque continued to say, "If Your Majesty consents to placing his royal stamp of approval on these official documents giving Peter La Ruche, my former first mate, lawful ownership of properties stolen from him by his enterprising stepbrother who incidentally had been in cahoots with the presiding court minister at the time, Pierre Fuquay, I dare say, it will facilitate matters considerably."

During the process of signing and embossing the papers Lafitte had set before him, Charles asked, "What do you propose to do about Philippe?"

With a hint of arrogance in his voice, Jacques said, "If my men and I had little difficulty in storming *your* palace, I should think finding a loophole in your brother's security would be hardly a chore."

"But Philippe is scheduled to leave for England any day now."

"Have faith, Your Majesty, Philippe will indeed soon leave for England, however, he will not get very far."

"I don't understand."

"It is a king who needs to come to terms with a king, not a prince. With your permission, my men and I will intercept your brother soon after he leaves his citadel, and it will be *you* settling the score with Henry, not he. That is, if you have strength enough to make the journey to England."

Charles contemplated for a moment and then said, "So be it. I concede that if Louie is to fulfill his destiny, I must exercise whatever power remains within me to see that it comes to fruition. However, Monsieur Lafitte, I assure you, nothing will deter me from attending Catherine's forthcoming memorial service at Saint Monica's Cemetery, and, I mean *nothing*."

Seizing the bell on his escritoire, Charles rang it vigorously and shouted, "Truffaut, dismiss my council members who have just reconvened. Tell them I'm off to see Sir Henry and that I'm no longer interested in hearing what any of them has to say. Pack my traveling clothes at once."

27

Recap of Events

Before Jacques Lafitte could effectively carry out his plan, it was imperative for him to persuade Charles to alter his itinerary pertaining to Catherine's memorial ceremony. In addition to this, since Lafitte was in haste to leave for Fontainebleau, the papers Charles had signed regarding Quicksand's estate needed to be served to the current landowner by Malcolm de Salle without delay. Prince Philippe's prearranged meeting with King Henry also had to be thwarted, and above all else, Louie's future assent to the Throne of France could not be compromised. To ensure his safety, until it was convenient to temporarily remove him from the palace to an undisclosed venue for protection, several of Lafitte's men kept a close vigil over him. Meanwhile Claude Truffaut, despite what Charles had directed him to say, informed the cabinet ministers that the king found it necessary to postpone their conference. Without explaining to him why, Bevier Lamont had been instructed by Lafitte to ready the stable horses for transportation.

The King of France, conscious of his obligation to Louie, agreed to all but one of Lafitte's precautious mandates, his impending visit to Saint Monica's Cemetery. Obstinate as he was, Charles insisted upon attending Catherine's annual memorial service. His persistence, however, finally yielded in a compromise. Because of the tenuous circumstances besieging him, His Majesty complied to attend a predawn ritual with Louie the next morning several days before the event was scheduled to take place. The newly affixed wreath alongside Catherine's tomb would hardly be noticed by anyone paying homage to their deceased queen.

Jacques Lafitte maintained a rigorous uphill climb to accomplish all the precarious items on his overwhelming agenda. Soon after the close of Catherine's privately held service, armed with the necessary documents, Malcolm de Salle, Quicksand, and a contingent of Charles's gendarmes set out for Sable Farms, the properties which once belonged to Peter La Ruche.

While King Charles, Cassis Yates (Lafitte's former boatswain) and a contingent of the Swiss Guard set out for Versailles, Jacques and Muslim Green (Lafitte's former quartermaster), accompanied by a large complement of gendarmes, galloped southward in the direction of Fontainebleau. Hoping his traitorous brother had been seized in time; Charles would patiently then wait on his ship until Lafitte showed up at the docks with Philippe in tow.

* * *

To Jacques Lafitte's jubilation, His Imperial Majesty had entertained the threats against France and her royal family with a renewed determination to vigorously oppose anyone who'd dare challenge the Throne's authority. To prevent anything from standing in the way of Louie's succession, it was Charles, with Lafitte's support, who ultimately decided to initiate the terms in settling matters with Philippe and Henry.

28

Justice Served

When Malcolm de Salle and a platoon of gendarmes arrived at the door of Monsieur Blanchford, the landowner said, "Who are you? What is it you want?"

"Monsieur, my name is unimportant. For the moment, let's just say I am a barrister of the high court and represent my client who, for the time being, shall remain anonymous."

"State your business and get out. Better yet, get out now, or I'll have you thrown out." Reaching for a nearby servant's bell for assistance, the host of Sable Farms recoiled at the strong grasp of Malcolm de Salle's grip.

"I wouldn't do that, Monsieur Blanchford. What I came here to say is of grave importance. If I don't receive your full cooperation, the inevitability that you will be duly executed in less than a fortnight by order of the king is most probable."

"This is an outrage. I've done nothing wrong."

"Perhaps not recently, but twenty years ago, according to these documents, you committed a felonious crime against my client who seeks immediate restitution."

"The king shall hear of this!"

"Monsieur, it is the king who sent me here. Do you not recognize his personal guard?"

"I too have a personal guard."

"Be careful of what you say, Cecil. May I call you, Cecil?"

"Get to the point. What is it you want of me?"

"I have irrevocable proof that all the properties of estate indicated in these documents have been illegally accessed by you and your former attorneys. In fact, my client has spent considerable time in prison for attempting to rebuke your claim of ownership to his estate."

"I'm supposed to believe all this? Your client, he has a name?"

"Yes, his name is Quicksand."

"Quicksand you say, I don't know anyone by that name."

"He's hoping, after hearing an offer you can hardly refuse, this entire issue can be settled out of court. You see, while in the process of stealing my client's inheritance, you robbed Peter La Ruche twenty irreplaceable years of his life, not to mention what you've done to his dignity."

"Peter La Ruche, my stepbrother? So he's behind all this."

Quicksand standing alongside de Salle removed his corsair's hat and said, "At your service, dear Stepbrother."

While Cecil remained speechless, the unidentified barrister said, "I have signed affidavits stating that Monsieur Pierre Fuquay gave you rightful claim to these properties."

"Splendid, Monsieur Fuquay's signatures exonerate me."

"No, Cecil, to the contrary, they have condemned you."

"How so? He was the official court administrator at the time."

"His Majesty, Charles, in recognizing Pierre Fuquay for the dastardly traitor he was, undoubtedly you attended his execution, could never officially proclaim after he uncovered the truth about him, that his former Treasury Minister had ever been telling the truth about anything. Your scheme would have worked, Monsieur, had Peter La Ruche failed in his courage to survive the beastly torments of the Bastille."

Blanchford remained quiescent. Quicksand approached him and said, "For your cussed behavior, dear Stepbrother, you deserve to die. But I'll give you a choice. Either you sign the papers giving me lawful ownership to Sable Farms . . ." Pausing, he withdrew a sword from its sheath and continued to say, "Or I will sever your head from your neck right now."

Without further ado, Monsieur Cecil Blanchford picked up the quill from its holder, dipped it into a well of ink, and scribbled his signature on the documents that had been designed to divest him of everything he had stolen. Pushing the papers in de Salle's direction, Blanchford said in a huff, "You haven't heard the last of this." He then abruptly stood up.

"Sit down!" Malcolm said in an authoritative voice.

"What more of me do you want? I've done as you asked."

Following Lafitte's instructions, Quicksand chimed in, "I believe there's a matter of restitution that needs to be paid—say, twenty years worth?"

Malcolm de Salle, having once been a former prison master of the Bastille, spoke teasingly, "Though I have not seen it myself, I happen to know the precise cell that best befits you. It's located toward the extreme end of the dungeon's lower level—the one where rats freely come and go as they please. Mounted to the chamber's iron clad door, so I've been told, there's an old familiar biblical saying. Perhaps you've heard it before. It goes something like this. *Ye shall reap what ye shall sow.*"

Quicksand, wanting to have the last word, said, "I recall once hearing something quite similar to it, Stepbrother. *Every man will receive, sooner or later, what's coming to him.*"

29

Change of Plan

When word from one of Philippe's informants reached him that Charles learned of his brother's assassination plot against the Throne and that of his intentions to conspire with Henry, the Prince of Fontainebleau became extremely furious. He immediately sent for his Lieutenant general, Anton Chambier. With his irate temper at a peak, Philippe scowled, "You and I were the only persons cognizant of my scheduled journey to England. What do you have to say for yourself?"

Somewhat perplexed, Anton said, "Say? Say about what, Your Grace?"

"Charles knows everything!"

"But that's impossible. Surely you don't believe I—"

Philippe abruptly silenced him. "You fool, with whom have you been consorting?" Chambier, shocked in disbelief to what he just heard, remained speechless.

"How often have I warned you not to mix duty with pleasure? What other interesting tidbits have you confided in Mademoiselle Van dermal? Never mind. My resourceful brother has already learned enough to hang us both."

Anton endeavored to speak. "Your Lordship, I—"

Philippe once again interrupted him with a caustic remark, "It was your harlot who loosened your tongue, wasn't it?"

Mortified, Chambier said, "Forgive me, Your Lordship, but I cannot recall ever mentioning anything about the matter of which you speak to Lissette."

"Once the wine reaches the loins, a man will say almost anything, especially when in the embrace of a scintillating traitor such as Mademoiselle Van dermal."

Anton, unable to defend his guilt in the matter, said, "What do you propose to do, Your Eminence?"

"There's still time. Henry will listen to reason. We leave for England at once."

"Your coach will be ready within the hour."

"Good, instead of taking the land route to Tourcoing, we'll ride to Versailles. Send a messenger ahead to secure a ship that will take us directly to Dover."

Feeling much less intimidated by his prince, Chambier said, "At once, Your Grace, but what about—"

"Your mistress? Not to worry, Anton, I've already taken care of *that* loose end."

30

Clash of Forces

As Lafitte and Philippe's forces were traveling full speed toward one another, their paths crossed midway between Paris and Fontainebleau. Anton, who had been asked to escort his prince to the outskirts of Versailles before making his final arrangements to assassinate the Royal Family, met Jacques's contingent head-on. Whereupon he and Lafitte drew their swords, the skirmish began. Steel clanged upon steel. Prince Philippe remained in his carriage. Slipping a pistol from his waistcoat, he then waited for an opportune moment to shoot down the corsair who was twice the fighter as his opponent.

While the two primary swordsmen twisted and turned in combat, Philippe raised his firearm and took careful aim at Lafitte. His moment of opportunity soon produced itself. In the process of parrying with his adversary, Jacques took a step backward. Catching his foot on a loose stone, Lafitte fell to the ground precisely the same moment Philippe's weapon discharged. As Chambier was about to thrust his sword into Jacques, who had dropped his weapon, the pellet caught Anton in the chest, killing him outright. It was then Philippe's outnumbered corsairs threw down their weapons and surrendered.

Brushing himself off, Lafitte shouted to Muslim Green, "I'm certain Charles will be delighted to hear that his brother was considerate enough to deliver himself right into our hands. We best be away immediately."

One of Lafitte's combatants hopped up on the carriage and seized control of the reins. Philippe demanded, "Where are you taking me?"

It was the quick-witted Muslim Green who answered, "To your brother Charles of course, or would you rather me run you through with my sword, Your Eminence?"

31

Brother to Brother

In the process of preparing to leave on his voyage for England, Charles had mixed feelings upon seeing his brother bound by ropes as Lafitte escorted him to the bridge of His Majesty's ship. The brief one-sided conversation took place moments after Philippe was forced to his knees, as though he was willfully paying proper homage to his king.

Charles said, "If you utter a single word while I am speaking, your tongue will instantly be severed from your mouth. Nod your head, if what I just said is clearly understood." Philippe promptly nodded with an affirmative gesture.

"The contempt I have for you, my disloyal brother, is beyond description. Either you surrender to me the names of all the informants you've inveigled against the Crown, or accept the consequences of being tossed into the sea, just as you are, before my crossing to England has been completed. If you wish to comply with this only request I demand of you, bow your head twice."

After Philippe once again gave Charles an affirmative response, the king said, "If ever there was an evil seed in our lineage, it is you, my dear brother, who have bested us all." Then, looking away, Charles said to no one in particular, "Take this prince of darkness to where he can do no more harm, a place where it will be impossible for him to inflict any further venomous threats upon the Crown."

* * *

Just before the king's ship was to set sail, Charles inquired about Louie's situation. Lafitte assured him that provisions had been made for the young prince to be taken to Sable Farms under the adequate protection of Peter La Ruche and his able comrades until it had been made safe for Louie to return to the palace.

"I must rest now," Charles said to Lafitte, "but not until I've considered the proper terms in explaining to Henry that all along he was in the right, whereas, it was I who was in the wrong."

Lafitte said, "Sire, I suggest you first restore your strength. I'm quite confident when the time approaches, you'll think of something most fitting to say to Lord Henry. I'll be sure to wake you the moment your ship nears Dover Point."

Before the king turned to enter his cabin, he said, "You mean, *Dantes Revenge*, it has a nice ring to it." It was then Jacques Lafitte knew in his heart that the bond he'd hoped to make with Charles was complete. Without having to say, if it ever came to it, he'd lay down his life for him.

32

Charles and Henry

Part I

As the entourage entered the receiving room at Dover Castle, Jacques Lafitte couldn't help but notice the cringe on Sir Henry's face when Charles, his nemesis, not Philippe, appeared before him. The King of France spoke first.

"Your Majesty, there simply wasn't time to forewarn you that there was a sudden change of plans. You see, my brother—for health reasons—decided to no longer entertain the prospect of becoming my successor."

"On the contrary, Sir Charles, after carefully reconsidering Philippe's amusing proposal, I realized that he'd end up being more of a thorn in my side than you could ever be." Lifting a newly inscribed dispatch addressed to Philippe from his table, he continued to say, "Here, read this. Perhaps then you'll believe I'm not as naive as you may perceive me to be."

Totally disinterested in perusing the contents of Henry's communiqué, Charles said, "I've not come here to question Your Eminence's privilege in making alliances with whomever you please."

"Oh," pointing to a chair, Henry said, "please make yourself comfortable, Uncle. I hope the winds that brought you to England's humble shores were favorable ones. However, I'm inclined to believe you've not come all this way to merely pay her king a social visit." Signaling to one of his attendants, he then said, "Food and wine for our honored guests."

Charles was more exhausted than in need of sustenance. France's ailing king hoped he had enough strength to settle matters with his pretentious nephew amicably. Lafitte, who had assumed the role of Minister of Foreign Affairs, simply crossed his fingers in hope that Charles would not collapse before the session had been completed.

33

Charles and Henry

Part II

"Whatever else there is for us to discuss, Sir Henry, I suggest it wait until our dispute over the colonies is finally put to rest. Do you not agree?"

Partially turning his back on Charles, the King of England said, "Twenty-four dispatches, I've counted them, have crossed between us since I lodged my first protest accusing France of usurping its power by proclaiming to be hers that which rightfully belongs to the British Commonwealth. Your Eminence, we have nothing further to discuss—unless, that is, your regime is willing to acknowledge that the colonial properties in question were wrongfully seized by France and that they immediately be returned to England."

Charles signaled Jacques Lafitte to withdraw the scrolls which extended from the shoulder pouch he'd been carrying. Fearful that the sudden gesture may have been intended as an act of aggression upon the king, Henry's bodyguards instinctively drew their weapons.

Lafitte spoke in an unperturbed voice, "Gentlemen," he said, "I hardly doubt any of these map projections should cause anyone present to be unduly alarmed." Clearing away a few wine goblets, Jacques proceeded to secure one of the charts to the table.

Charles then said to Henry, who had impulsively turned around when the brief moment of intensity occurred, "Come, Your Majesty, let's have a look. With the able assistance of my newly appointed Minister of Foreign Affairs, Monsieur Lambert Dubois, I have sufficient reason to believe all is not what they had at one time appeared to be."

The two kings simultaneously approached the table where Lafitte's unfurled map lay before them. Charles pointed his index finger to a group of islands in an area southeast of the Bahamas. "This archipelago," he said, "was first sighted by Juan Ponce de Leon during the early fifteen hundreds. Never having established a settlement on either island, the Spanish passed them on to the French. We too, all this time, have failed to properly sustain firm control and departmental jurisdiction over the Turks and Caicos Islands as well."

Henry quickly perked up and declared, "This has been my precise point. These same properties are an extension of the Grand Bahamas, which in fact belong to England. Soon after France abandoned her efforts to secure proper claim to these two potential colonies, England immediately commenced procedures to annex them to be part of the greater strand of islands she already possessed."

Jacques Lafitte was amazed to see how each of the monarchs clearly articulated their viewpoints in explaining what neither of their representative Ministers of Foreign Affairs, prior to this occasion, could translate into common sense. The conversation appeared to be an honest, open revelation of facts, rather than an argumentative debate based on prejudicial opinions.

Charles looked at Henry and said, "One can readily see the quandary my former Minister of Foreign Affairs, Monsieur Stephan-Baptist Colbert, God rest his soul, must have found himself while attempting to connect the various departmental sovereignties in the Caribbean to the proper time lines relative to their discoveries. Your Liege, the moment the poor fellow shot himself during which time my cabinet and I were attempting to get to the truth of the matter, I can assure you it was not a pretty sight, I suddenly realized there had been more to what you were saying than what I was willing to believe. Mind you, I just recently received a dispatch from a neutral arbitrator to the colonies confirming that everything you inferred is completely in accordance with the law."

"Does this then indicate you are now willing to concede that the Turks and Caicos Islands rightfully belong to England?"

The chamber suddenly assumed an eerie silence. If the road to peace between France and England were ever to be rekindled, Charles needed to invoke an affirmative answer.

Charles finally said, "It appears, after giving the matter careful deliberation, I have no other choice but to surrender to the Commonwealth of England that which does not officially belong to France. Yes, Your Majesty, the Turks and Caicos Islands are yours."

Lafitte breathed a sigh of relief. However, when Henry insisted upon asking for more, Jacques's heart skipped a beat. "Charles, are you willing to concede to England the islands of Montserrat and Anguilla as well?"

"I was getting to that, Brother-in-law." Lafitte, without having to be coaxed, as though the present sequence of events had been preordained, unfolded a second chart depicting a chain of islands situated along the Lesser Antilles in the West Indies.

Feeling somewhat faint, Charles began to reach for the vial tucked inside his tunic. After steadying himself, he withdrew an empty hand from his garment. Lafitte proceeded to touch a finger to the islands on the parchment that were in question.

The King of France said, "Ah, yes, Montserrat and Anguilla—what have we here? If I've been informed correctly, after a brief skirmish with Spain, these two islands fell under British control. Later, during another of our forefather's feisty revolutions, France captured Montserrat. Somehow, Anguilla also became entangled in French colonial affairs. Be as it may, to my knowledge, neither of these colonies had ever been officially departmentalized by the Republic of France. If it pleases Your Majesty, and if it will once and for all bring an end to your superfluous dispatches, I relinquish Santa Maria de Montserrat and Anguilla to your safekeeping. Is there anything else required of me, Henry, before you are willing to certify a genuine peace between our sovereign nations?"

"No further requisitions are necessary. However, Brother-in-law, while the documents of our treaty are being drawn up, I'd like to set the record straight regarding age-old disconcerting rumors concerning my sister, Catherine."

"I'll be most obliging to do so, Sire, but not until you include in our treaty England's willingness to pay full restitution to France for the eight cargo ships that were sunk by your cannon wielding gun boats."

"Six cargo ships, you mean."

"Shall we compromise without further bickering and settle for seven cargo ships, Brother-in-law?"

"Now I know why Edward often referred to you as a conniving rascal, Charles. Seven it is."

34

Charles and Henry

Part III

Though he did not outwardly show it, the King of France was excitedly happy with the way his and Henry's discussion had ended with a peace treaty between their respective sovereign nations. As it turned out, Philippe's alliance with England was nothing more than a puff of smoke. Charles surmised that Henry had been under much parliamentary pressure and that it was in his best interest to keep the threat of war with France alive until he displayed to the world that England, despite her unpopularity, would remain a dominant force in Europe. Louie's succession to the throne, however, still needed to be addressed. If the young king's regime were to have Henry as an ally, and with Jacques Lafitte there to guide him, the garçon would indeed enhance his chances of being a noble ruler of France.

Charles sat back in a comfortable armchair and patiently waited for the final touches of the peace treaty to be presented to him for his perusal and signature. Once it became an official document, he'd no longer feel that his royal administration had been a total failure. While Charles contemplated how his tenure as King, without Catherine by his side to sustain him, was nothing more than a reign of terror, he noticed Henry gazing at his older counterpart.

Charles said, "Your Majesty, exactly what is it you would like to hear about your sister? Ah, yes, now I recall the disconcerting rumors maligning the Queen of France."

"All these years, Charles, I wondered whether Catherine indeed had been traipsing around the Caribbean with—what's the dastardly renegade's name?"

"Sir Henry, I believe the swashbuckler you're referring to goes by the nomen Lafitte, Jacques Lafitte."

"Is it true the Queen of France had the unpropitious audacity to chase after this roguish knave?"

"Rumors, Your Grace, all rumors. To set the record straight, Catherine had been on a goodwill mission at the time she sailed to Martinique. Her only oversight was not informing me of her sudden aspiration to voyage the high seas. Incidentally, as I recall, your father offered me at least ten galleons to insure her safe return."

"I suppose you blame me for not fulfilling his wishes."

"Before we go into that, I can only tell you that whatever became of this infamous privateer remains a mystery. You see, he has a variety of aliases which are indeed most difficult to monitor. However, this I can assure you, if the scoundrel ever dared so much to show his face in all Europe, I'd have him hanged and quartered for all France to see." Lafitte, who was attentively listening to Charles's commentary, instinctively choked at what he just heard.

Henry, quite amused, said, "It appears you and I, Charles, have managed to reach an agreement on this matter as well. Perhaps we do think alike after all."

Charles spoke frankly. "Henry, I am not in a position to question another king's decisions. In any event, I doubt very much that the ships Edward promised me would have significantly helped the situation. This, however, I think you should know. Your sister often spoke highly of you. Catherine believed she'd been the cause of the rift that developed between you and Edward. Is it not so, Henry, the King of England doted on his princess more than his heir to the throne?"

Henry did not answer. Charles said, "Catherine confided in me that your father implored your sister several times to accept my proposal of marriage. England needed an ally, and Edward sorely needed to make amends for the countless years he neglected in spending quality time with his beloved prince."

As his eyes began to blur, Henry said, "And you married Catherine knowing she didn't love you?"

"It is indescribable to explain in mere words the ecstasy that enraptured me the very moment I laid eyes on her. Upon our first encounter, I knew immediately that having Catherine for my queen meant more to me than the alliance your father proposed with England and France."

Though internally moved by what Charles said, Henry needed to settle a sensitive subject which the King of France would find most difficult in attempting to justify. What better time to do it than the present?

35

Charles and Henry

Part IV

For the exception of Charles, what the King of England said next completely flabbergasted anyone in the vast chamber close enough to have heard his forthcoming exchange of words. Whether Henry was attempting to provoke Charles, or simply interested in learning the truth, he spoke in a controlled voice, "Shortly after Edward died, I received a dispatch that you publicly accused me at one of your open house extravaganzas that I deliberately had my father killed while he slept in his bed. Tell me it isn't true, Sire. I have witnesses willing to lay down their lives in swearing to uphold what they've heard."

"Henry, you should know above all else whenever a king says anything during an informal festive occasion, there's very little truth to be gained in what his lips impart, especially after he exceeds his normal ration of vintage wine. Yes, Your Grace, to my dismay, I did utter such words. For what it's worth, soon afterward, I did recant the accusation. However, as you know, in an unforgiving world, ill-spoken words tend to ring louder than repentant ones."

"At least now you have a greater insight as to why I despised you so."

"To think, save for the carelessness of a single slip of the tongue, we could have been inseparable allies all these years."

The inscribers of the newly drawn treaty entered the room and set the documents before Charles. After the King of France perused them, he picked up a quill, and before scratching his signature on the parchment, he said, "If it means anything, Henry, I am totally convinced you had nothing to do with Edward's death. His entire life clamored for peace. As I see it, in spite of some of your past indiscretions, today you have chosen to follow in His Lordship's footsteps."

36

Charles and Henry

Part V

With official business having been concluded, Henry, satisfied with the proceedings, said, "Your Majesty, I believe this is your first trip to England. Won't you accept my hospitality and stay a few days? There's much to see, and I'm sure you will not be disappointed."

"As much as I'd fancy to see where Catherine and you grew up in the country gardens she often alluded to, it's best I . . ." Charles leaned forward and practically fell into Henry's arms. "As you can see, my present condition will not permit me such luxury."

While Henry called for a litter, Jacques Lafitte and one of the king's attendants supported Charles. Steadying himself, the King of France reached into his pocket and withdrew an item he endeared most preciously. Slipping it into Henry's hand, he said, "Sire, this fleur-de-lis was given to me by your father as a token of friendship on the day Catherine and I exchanged our betrothals. At a time I desperately needed his assistance, I sent it to him by courier with a message to meet with me at specified coordinates in the English Channel."

Henry examined the solid gold charm while Charles continued speaking. "Moments before our brief encounter had been concluded, your father returned the token of friendship I had sent to him. I recall his exact words: *I believe this belongs to you*, he said. Henry, I bring this to your attention for the sole purpose of letting you know that Edward and I disagreed on a number of issues. However, not once did it ever occur to either of us that we should wage war against one another in spite of our differences. Soon after Edward died, I came to realize what a fool I've been for not recognizing the greatness His Lordship truly possessed in attempting to combat England's most formidable enemies."

"Charles, would you care to elaborate? Which of his adversaries had my father been referring to?"

"Poverty, bigotry, disloyalty, and the right to publicly profess one's personal religious beliefs were just a few of the thorns giving your father consternation. Edward was also dismayed that his ministerial staff deemed it necessary to levee taxes on those who could least afford to pay them. Unfortunately, he died before"—Charles once again hesitated—"before he could implement the humane changes His Majesty intended to enforce."

It was obvious to those around him that Charles was failing rapidly. He said to Henry, "I ask you to consider only this, Sire. Regard the token of friendship your father extended to me on the *Monticello* as a symbol of solidarity between our two sovereign nations. Perhaps one day you will celebrate with France's new king, my son, the sentiments of enduring peace which Edward had proposed to me nearly seventeen years ago."

Charles began to breathe heavily. As he was slowly being carried through the castle's huge entranceway, he motioned for the entourage to halt. Finding it unbearable to speak, France's waning King tugged on Henry's tunic. Drawing closer, he heard Charles say in a voice slightly above a whisper, "Henry, the moment I breathe my last, Louie will embrace you in being his closest ally."

"Your Majesty, isn't that for him to decide?"

"I'm confident he already has. You're his only last hope of capturing whatever can be recalled of his mother's earlier years. It would mean so much to the garçon, if you gave Catherine a freshly painted face by describing to him the many wondrous tales the two of you shared as siblings with an awesome grandfather that he'd been deprived of ever having been acquainted. Louie, upon hearing of my journey to see you, insisted that I ask you to accept his humble invitation to ride with him. After my young prince becomes King, do not be surprised at his gesture to return the favor of your father by sending his uncle in England the most splendid thoroughbreds France has to offer."

Very much moved by Charles's words, Henry said, "Thank you, Your Majesty, for opening my eyes to issues I'd been unable to bring to closure without the insight that only your intuitive perception could provide." With a contrite heart, the King of England whispered softly in Charles's ear, "To think, I've permitted avarice, misery, contempt, and the lust for an insignificant group of remote islands to blind my better judgment. Be most assured, Your Grace, my nephew will never grow tired in asking me anything he wants to learn about his mother, for I have many precious stories that will keep him forever curiously amused."

Although Henry suspected Charles had not much more time to live, he returned the ailing monarch's *"Bonjour, Henry"* with "May God see you safely back to France, Charles, and yes, tell my nephew I'll be most honored to have a speedy gallop with France's future king."

37

Jacques Lafitte's Dilemma

Henry's prediction came sooner than had been anticipated. Prior to his ship reaching the shores of France, Charles was stricken with a massive heart attack and died.

Jacques Lafitte did not have much time to consider the consequences that were sure to follow. He wondered if Louie had been strong enough to absorb the shock and maintain the leadership role required of him to rule France in the manner Catherine had often prayed he would.

At the close of a brief memorial service on the foredeck of the king's ship, before seeing to it that Charles was adequately prepared for the fleeting journey ahead, Lafitte summoned Muslim Green and Cassis Yates to return the corpse to his cabin. Although what he needed to do next appeared unthinkable, somehow his mates understood and went about in silence doing their captain's bidding. Whether or not it was the right thing to do, Lafitte proceeded to follow the dictates of his conscience. Invoking a supplication to the Almighty, he prayed, "Your Supreme Majesty, let the quandary in which I've placed myself evermore forsake me not."

When everything was in readiness, Jacques commenced the writing of a missive to Louie in Charles's name. It began, *To My Beloved Prince* . . .

* * *

Darkness had fallen upon Paris when the royal carriage transporting Charles's cadaver passed through the palace gates. The coach, accompanied by Jacques's entourage impersonating Swiss guardsmen, was permitted to enter without being halted at Lafitte's boisterous intonation, "Open, in the name of the king. Make way for His Majesty, the king!"

Anticipating his worst imaginings, Truffaut was terrified at the dejected look on Jacques's face. "Claude," he said, "Charles is dead."

"Come with me, monsieur, we've much to do before daybreak. However, before I am to fulfill His Majesty's final mandates, according to his verbal wishes, had I the good fortune to outlive him, I must first indulge myself in a glass of brandy prior to whatever else I must do. Under the circumstances, won't you join me in a toast to our beloved deceased king?"

While Lafitte and Truffaut celebrated the king's passing with a glass of wine, Jacques was informed that Charles insisted, at the time of his death, he be expeditiously interred without public fanfare in the mausoleum reserved for the royal couple. Muslim Green, prompted by Lafitte, swiftly galloped to Sable Farms to whisk Prince Louie and the others back to the palace. At the same hour, Catherine's remains were exhumed from the Rose Garden and prepared for immediate transfer to Saint Monica's Cemetery where all France had believed her to be all this time.

It was just after daybreak when the brief unobtrusive ceremony had been concluded. Prince Louie, Bevier, Claude, Gilbert, Jacques, and several of his mates were in attendance. The great tomb, according to the king's wishes, was hermetically sealed—thus locking in all its secrets. Though the people of France frowned upon the fact that Charles died and was interred without receiving proper homage, they soon diverted their undivided attention to the fast-approaching royal festivities regarding Prince Louie's anticipated ascent to the throne.

* * *

The aforementioned turn of events happened so quickly that Louie, unable to come to terms with all that had recently transpired, sent for Monsieur Lambert Dubois. If he were indeed to be inaugurated King, France's steward, a particular matter that deeply disturbed Louie had first needed to be resolved to his complete satisfaction. It had something to do with what he had overheard during a spirited conversation Charles and Monsieur Dubois were having in his father's reception room.

38

Lafitte and Louie

Part I

It was to be a great day for France. Everything was in readiness. King Henry's unexpected appearance to attend Prince Louie's Coronation Ceremony added a flurry of excitement to an already ecstatic multitude of well-wishers. The prescribed mourning period for Charles had barely concluded when the announcement had come that his son, Louie, born of Catherine, bore no impediments—thus giving him lawful succession to the throne of France. Hours before the ritual was to take place, however, the adolescent prince called Monsieur Lambert Dubois to the very same room Charles had often used to conduct official business. What he said to him came as a total surprise—one that would change the course of history, depending upon the outcome of their exchange of words.

Amazingly, Louie's first utterances sounded much like that of a seasoned king. He said, "Monsieur, I command that you hold your tongue until you are asked to speak. Is that clearly understood?"

Dubois, completely taken aback, was about to say, *"Yes, Your Majesty,"* but decided instead to nod his head with a slight affirmative bow.

Louie's voice changed abruptly. It was soft and remorseful. "I believe it is my moral duty to abdicate the Throne of France even before I take the oath of office. And I shall tell you why, Monsieur Dubois, or is it Monsieur Murielle, or maybe I'm addressing at the moment, Monsieur Giles, whom I once endeared to be my faithful stable confidant? No, I believe you are none of the above. Tell me with a simple yes or a simple no—which is it to be—*or* are you not indeed Captain Jacques Lafitte, the same man that fathered me as his son?"

Dumbfounded upon hearing this, Lafitte had to think quickly. Louie somehow discovered the truth of Jacques's masquerading antics and understandably was looking for a suitable explanation. However, a mere misspoken word would completely unravel everything Jacques Lafitte hoped to accomplish in fulfilling Catherine's wishes. "Yes and no, Your Majesty" was his reply.

Louie's face assumed a perplexed look. He then said, "I'd appreciate very much if you'd explain what you mean by *yes and no*, monsieur."

"Yes, Your Majesty, I indeed fit the description of all the aforementioned gentlemen you just alluded to, and no, in all fairness I cannot malign Charles's integrity by proclaiming you as my birth son."

"Then perhaps you'd kindly clarify what I had overheard you and"—Louie could not bring himself to say Father—"you and Charles had been bickering about at the time we first met. Before you say anything, allow me to refresh your memory."

Louie went over to the courtyard window, as Charles had often done at such times the thought of Catherine crossed his mind. Stretching his neck to get a better glimpse of the Rose Garden, he proceeded to say, "Mind you, I was not intentionally eavesdropping. After all, the conversation was quite deafening. Surely, monsieur, you do recall verbatim the incident in question. *I* most certainly can. How is it possible for me to forget? It took place in this very chamber. I distinctly remember Charles interrupting our tête-à-tête. You and I were discussing Mother's Caribbean adventure. He said, 'Louie, will you be so kind to tell Monsieur Truffaut to inform the members of my council that I will be rejoining them momentarily?'"

The prince diverted his attention from the window. He said, "I hadn't gotten very far when I realized I left my book of verses on the settee. There was something in it I wanted Monsieur Truffaut to see. Upon returning to retrieve it, I overheard you and Charles having a heated dialogue. You were informing him that you'd rather lay down your life before ever proclaiming me to be your son and that my mother asked you to promise her you'd look after me. Fortunate for me, the door was closed. If you had seen how I reacted to what you were saying, you would have thought you'd seen a ghost."

Louie then meekly added, "You needn't lie to me, Monsieur Lafitte. If I'm to be King, I must first know who I truly am. If I am not the son of Charles, then according to the Rite of Succession, it would be dishonest for me to embrace the Throne of France, when in fact, I am not its rightful heir."

39

Lafitte and Louie

Part II

Jacques Lafitte's response to Prince Louie, if it were to be effective in coercing him to reconsider following through with the monumental gesture he had just proposed, spontaneously said, "Oh that, you mean to say His Majesty never clued you in on his devious scheme?"

"What scheme?"

"They say Solomon was a wise king. Personally I believe your father, in some ways, was a tad wiser."

"What has King Solomon to do with any of this?"

"Wisdom, Your Grace, wisdom." Daring to move closer to Louie, Lafitte gently placed a hand on the boy's shoulder. "Prior to your first meeting with Monsieur Dubois, His Majesty had called upon me to assist him with a grave matter that had constantly been gnawing at his heart and soul."

"What matter?"

"My Prince, you leave me no choice but to discharge secrets that were never intended to ever again be uttered by anyone. The matter which gave Charles much anguish was your ever-recurring nightmarish dreams. According to your father, the physicians lost all hope in attempting to find a cure for whatever it was that precipitated your terrifying nighttime hallucinations. He contemplated over and over again that there had to be a rational solution in resolving your dilemma."

"Such as?"

"The deceptive scheme I previously alluded to dawned on Charles shortly after my"—Dubois corrected himself—"shortly after Jacques Lafitte's sudden appearance electrified your father into thinking yours truly was an apparition. He wanted to know why I disobeyed his royal command by returning to France before locating His Majesty's lost treasure. Having grown weary of the interminable search, I had explained to him that my crew and I sailed back to our homeland with the hope of being granted His Lordship's merciful pardon."

Pretending to be deep in thought, Lafitte commenced to pace the floor. "It so happened," he said, "Charles's attention had been focused on more important matters. I believe the notion had suddenly occurred to him that I could be of great service to him and that's when he gave my crew and me a most heartwarming reprieve. Toward the end of our conversation, His Majesty asked me to join with him in carrying out his intuitive plan. After hearing him out, I heartily agreed to abide by his wishes. The opportunity to implement His Majesty's scheme coincidentally came sooner than expected when you entered the room. If you recall, at the time, we were not engaged in a verbal spat."

Lafitte clearly could see he had Prince Louie's undivided attention. "My prince," he said, "try to recollect the precise moment you and I were discussing your mother's adventures on the high seas. It was then Charles, sensing you placed yourself in a vulnerable position, seized the opportunity to implement his plan. His Majesty deliberately interrupted our conversation by asking you to deliver a message to Monsieur Truffaut. Knowing you'd be anxious to hear more about your mother's journey to the Caribbean, we crossed our fingers and prayed that you would soon return."

"Continue," Louie said, "what happened then?"

"When Charles and I were certain you were at the door, we commenced raising our voices, as though we'd been arguing since you left the room. It was at that point you overheard me say that I'd rather lay down my life before proclaiming you to be my son. Think, Louie, if the queen asked me to promise her that I'd look after you, my own son, why on God's earth would I wait sixteen years to fulfill her wishes? Don't you see the row your father and I were having was intended to shock you? Naturally, in order to convince you we were at wit's end, the atmosphere needed to be ignited with rancor and bitter rage."

Completely engrossed in what he was hearing, Louie said, "And?"

"It was a mere chance in ten thousand, but Charles sincerely believed that the essence of our thunderous exchange of words might just be disturbing enough for your subconscious grief-stricken mind to trigger a release in exorcising whatever demons had been binding your night dreams in a capsule of fear during which time your mother had been under an inexorable emotional strain at the time of your birth. Yes, Louie, in the hope of shaking the devil's sentinels right out of you, Charles would do anything, even if it meant losing the priceless affection a son held in such high esteem for his father."

Louie reflected for a few moments on Lafitte's last words. He then said, "How could either of you have known I was outside the door? You see I was wearing my favorite shoes that day, the soles of which are lined with a velvety cushion."

"Sire, it wasn't your footsteps that warned us of your presence, it was the decorative bells on your tunic that alerted Charles and me that his scheme needed to go into effect without further ado."

Reaching into his pocket, Lafitte withdrew a sealed envelope. Handing it to Louie, he said, "I intended to give this to you after your coronation, but I think you should read it now. Perhaps then you'll better understand how much His Majesty truly loved his son and the great lengths he'd go through in making certain nothing stood in the way of your succession to the throne of France."

Prince Louie pondered for a brief moment before he opened the letter. Admittedly, the incident the two had been discussing did take place within the precise timeline during which his diabolic hallucinations unexplainably came to an abrupt halt. Somewhat mystified, the young prince, still plagued with skepticism, proceeded to break the seal of the communiqué. Removing the letter, he began to read it.

40

Lafitte and Louie

Part III

Louie elected to read Charles's letter aloud. The missive had no date. It began:

To My Beloved Prince,
　Forgive me for deserting my dear son at a time he needed me to be more of a father than a king. My business with Lord Henry could not be postponed any longer. Your uncle is not such a bad chap after all. We've settled our differences (it's all in the treaty), and he's anxiously awaiting your invitation to have a gallop or two in the near future.
　Son, you can see that I am extremely weak. My handwriting is barely legible. Know only this, my prince,

the happiest day in Catherine's life and mine was when you came into this world. Because I was unable to be in attendance for the occasion, it was also one of your father's saddest days of his life.

There is so much my heart would like to impart to you, special memories which I had hoped to share with you while we promenaded together in the Rose Garden. I know one day you will fulfill your mother's most ardent wish—to be France's noblest King. To be sure, it is mine as well.

Louie, I implore you to accept the bearer of this letter into your confidence—to be your obedient servant, just as Monsieur Truffaut had been to me. I know him quite well. It was he who endeavored to save your mother from the torments of her ordeal while at sea.

I love you, my son. May the heavens above shower you with spiritual guidance and mortal protection.

+ Father +

Wanting desperately to believe that the letter he held was in fact written by Charles—with tears streaming down his cheeks—Louie stammered and said, "Monsieur Lafitte, can you so-sol . . . solemnly swear upon all that is good and holy, including all those you have dearly loved, that what I have just read was positively scripted by the hand of whom you say is my father, Charles, the recently deceased King of France?"

It was obvious to Prince Louie that Jacques Lafitte was taken aback by what he just heard. He wondered for a moment if it was because the question he asked seemed impertinent to the gentleman standing before him, or was it simply because he could not in all honesty give an affirmative answer.

As Lafitte retrieved a handkerchief from his sleeve to pat away the moisture that had accrued on his cheeks, in a flash, his mind reverted back to when he instructed Muslim Green and Cassis Yates to return Charles's lifeless body to His Majesty's cabin. What transpired at that time may be construed as diabolical or even a sacrilegious outrage. However, for Louie's sake, Jacques Lafitte needed to bring to a definitive close all that had entangled him to the Royal Family. Perhaps it was Catherine's spirit once again urging him to act as he did. Or was it something from within his heart that prompted him to right the wrong he had committed a long, long time ago? He really couldn't be sure. This much he did know. Just to live in his son's shadow would be enough not to want for anything more.

Without questioning their captain's motive, Lafitte's mates followed his instructions with meticulous precision. While Charles held the quill in his hand, he precariously leaned to one side on Lafitte's lap. With the able assistance of his two entrusted shipmates, Jacques unhesitatingly scrawled the farewell letter of a King to his son.

"Your Majesty," Jacques finally spoke up," I swear to you upon all that is good and holy, and upon the graves of all those I ever loved and was loved by, it was Charles's hand that scripted the very letter you are presently holding in your hands. So help me God."

To Jacques Lafitte's total surprise, Prince Louie said, "Monsieur, are you not the least bit interested in learning how I found out about all your deceptive disguises?"

Lafitte humbly answered, "Whoever it was, Your Lordship, I'm inclined to believe it's one secret you'll never divulge."

"Perhaps one day I shall. If I'm to take you into my confidence, as Father strongly urged me to do, there mustn't be any secrets between us. Don't you agree?"

"Wholeheartedly, Sire, and now it's time for you to get dressed for your royal coronation. The moment of truth has arrived, the one your mother and father had envisioned for their precious son—to nobly lead the people of France into a new dawn where injustice, want, and poverty will not be tolerated."

"Monsieur Lafitte, of all your aliases, I liked Sir Giles the most. Therefore, from now on I shall address you Sir Giles. What I mean to say is, I'm no longer fearful of the duties that lay ahead, especially knowing you will always be there to guide me."

"I'll endeavor not to disappoint you, Your Majesty."

"Do you think I should don the blue sash or the gold one?"

"Your Majesty must remember that it is *you* who must ultimately decide, big or small, whatever decision best suits His Royal Highness."

"I think the blue sash will do fine. Father often told me it was the color of Mother's eyes."

Epilogue

King Charles and Jacques Lafitte had been inundated with a plethora of urgent matters at the outset of their first encounter. When the two converged, it didn't take very long for either of them to set aside their differences or find it necessary to relive the past. An unspoken agreement, that Prince Louie had been their prime concern, became evident when both men placed Catherine's son above all else. To the very end, action, not words, had become the order of the day.

It is fair to assume that had Lafitte not responded to Catherine's persistent spirit urging him back to France, Charles would have undoubtedly fallen prey to Philippe's fiendish assassination plot against the Crown. At the same token, Jacques, with the support of his crew, had made it possible to assist Charles in reconciling the king's dilemma with his archenemy, King Henry.

The actual sentence imposed on Prince Philippe by Charles is not of grave importance. It is solely left to the discretion of the reader to make a personal assumption as to what became of him.

The King of France learned quite soon after Catherine died that it was impossible for him to remarry. Charles could never relinquish the affection he had maintained for his deceased queen. Though His Majesty did not at first inwardly proclaim Louie to be his son, later, when the young prince began to mature, Charles saw in him much of that which reminded him of Catherine.

It would only be natural to assume Prince Louie's reign had been everything his mother had hoped for it to be. After all things considered, without fully realizing it, Louie did appoint his birth father, Jacques Lafitte, Minister of Foreign and Domestic Affairs to assist him in making prudent decisions during the lion's share of his tenure as the Royal King of France.

Peter La Ruche's newly acquired estate was evenly divided among any of his mates expressing a desire to settle there with their reunited families. Most of them, having been personally involved in maintaining Prince Louie's safety, accepted employment within the palace as the newly crowned King of France's personal guard.

As to be expected, the sands of time eventually ran its course for Monsieur Claude Truffaut, Monsieur Bevier Lamont, and Monsieur Gilbert Montclair whose contributions to the outcome of this story had been magnanimous.

It was some time after arriving in Paris with Malcolm de Salle to assist him that Lafitte finally managed to carry out each of the items he had crafted on his agenda. He often visited Leticia and Dantes Lafitte's places of interment. It was his stepfather who had not only given Louie Grapier a second lease on life but also groomed the orphan boy into becoming one of France's finest disciples. King Louie faithfully donned the ring Monsieur Giles explained once belonged to Catherine's mother. Whenever Sir Giles and his sire frequented Saint Monica's Cemetery, the token was always seen dangling on a chain the young king religiously wore around his neck.

King Louie visited Sable Farms whenever he could, especially when France's Favorite Son needed time to be just himself. It was there he met the future Queen of France. Antoinette was much like Catherine, his mother, who had grown up surrounded by England's peaceful countryside where the simple things in life were never taken for granted.

Author's Note

In the first and third books of my trilogy, I refrained from addressing any of the kings, princes, or Catherine with a surname or numerical identification title—the obvious reason being that, historically speaking, there would have been too many gross inconsistencies. The same holds true for specified time lines in which several of the Caribbean Colonies were actually claimed and settled by Europe's various sovereign nations.

Leviticus 20:26 tells us to be sacred, *"To me, therefore, you shall be sacred; for I, the Lord, am sacred, I, who have set you apart from the other nations to be my own."* How wonderful! To think, each of us is called to be His own and to be sacred.

None are alone in the fight against whatever it is that seeks to disturb one's inner peace. Consequently, it behooves each of us to place our trust in Him who has called us to be holy. Though at times it may be difficult to envision, is it not wiser to walk in the company of angels than to seek that which is fleeting and can never truly satisfy? However hopeless any of us may sometimes perceive ourselves to be, because our source of origin stems from an incomprehensible Power of Love, there's invariably imbedded in the heart of every sinner a seed of human kindness that is poised to sprout even at the unlikeliest of times.

To celebrate the conclusion of my trilogy, you who have shared your precious time with my characters in reading any one of my books will be remembered in a perpetual annual novena of masses. Let us praise the Lord together, as we go forth to do His bidding.